Look Both Ways

JACQUELYN MITCHARD

raz**O**r
bill

RAZORBILL
Published by the Penguin Group
Penguin Young Readers Group
345 Hudson Street, New York, New York 10014, U.S.A.
Penguin Group (USA) Inc., 375 Hudson Street, New York, New York 10014, U.S.A.
Penguin Group (Canada), 90 Eglinton Avenue East, Suite 700, Toronto, Ontario, Canada M4P 2Y3
(a division of Pearson Penguin Canada Inc.)
Penguin Books Ltd, 80 Strand, London WC2R 0RL, England
Penguin Ireland, 25 St Stephen's Green, Dublin 2, Ireland (a division of Penguin Books Ltd)
Penguin Group (Australia), 250 Camberwell Road, Camberwell, Victoria 3124, Australia
(a division of Pearson Australia Group Pty Ltd)
Penguin Books India Pvt Ltd, 11 Community Centre, Panchsheel Park, New Delhi – 110 017, India
Penguin Group (NZ), 67 Apollo Drive, Mairangi Bay, Auckland 1311, New Zealand
(a division of Pearson New Zealand Ltd)
Penguin Books (South Africa) (Pty) Ltd, 24 Sturdee Avenue, Rosebank, Johannesburg 2196,
South Africa
Penguin Books Ltd, Registered Offices: 80 Strand, London WC2R 0RL, England

All rights reserved. Copyright © 2009 Jacquelyn Mitchard
Library of Congress Cataloging-in-Publication Data
Mitchard, Jacquelyn. Look both ways / by Jacquelyn Mitchard. p. cm. Summary: When psychic twin
Mallory Brynn starts seeing imges of a white wildcat in her dreams, she tries to figure out the connection
of her images to an injured cheerleader and her Native American friend Eden.
ISBN 978-1-59514-161-3 (hardcover) [1. Twins--Fiction. 2. Sisters--Fiction. 3. Psychic abilities--
Fiction. 4. Cheerleading--Fiction. 5. Native Americans--Fiction.] I. Title. PZ7.M6848Lo 2009
[Fic]--dc22 2008028997
10 9 8 7 6 5 4 3 2 1
Printed in the United States of America

For Pamela English
What hearts your heart has touched

ONCE MORE INTO THE DREAM

ONCE MORE INTO THE DREAM

Great-grandpa Walker, ninety-two years old, always picked the darkest night to tell the stories. He rested his chin on the tent poles of his long fingers and said, "These hills have seen strange sights, you know. . . ."

Even the twins, teenagers Mallory and Meredith, the oldest of the Brynn grandchildren and technically past the days of campfire stories, couldn't help but shiver. As their father or Uncle Kevin piled the night's last dry logs onto the coals, the littlest cousins sat on their parents' laps and the older ones huddled in the blankets from the family cabins—blankets that would have felt stiff and scratchy at home but were somehow comforting up at the camp on Crying Woman Ridge. The fire painted Grandpa's strong, thin face with weird streaks of color as he painted word pictures of his own grandfather, Ellery, toiling up Canada Road with his wife and two children, his cooking pots and wooden roof shingles on the backs of five Welsh ponies. Before that, they'd sailed to New York in a packet boat off the wild coast of Wales, determined to scrape a living from the rich veins of copper beneath this rough land. They were Welsh miners, used to deprivation and harsh conditions, and so they prospered.

Ellery Brynn's first home was the many-times-updated cabin that still stood in the middle of the cabin camp—a house only a few hundred feet from the mine shaft he helped to build. But with his son and grandson, he helped found Ridgeline, the little town in the valley. There, he built five of the big brick foursquare houses on Pilgrim Road, and a Brynn son or daughter once lived in every one. Now, only Meredith and Mallory's father, Tim and his family lived in the house where Tim had grown up. Three of the other houses had been torn down, and one housed the town library. Still, their family's place in the town's past wasn't just a story; it was history.

But the tales Grandpa Walker told weren't written down in historical pamphlets or old documents.

They were ancient and strange. Long before carjackers or thieves who "picked your pockets clean," as Grandpa Walker put it, there were good reasons for children to nip up their heels and head home before dark. Black bears and mountain lions roamed the trails in these provinces just below Canada. Three times, a child had come up missing. His father's best friend was called Oberlin Bent Tree, a Cree Indian, and Oberlin's French wife, Regine, swore that one of those children was adopted by the lions—that she ran wild, brown and agile as the cubs, her long, long dark hair streaming. On cold spring moonlit nights, children would wake and rush through the partitions of cotton wool that served as walls to leap into their parents' beds when the mountain lions howled for their mates. It was a sound that seemed to pass through the walls of the sturdy log houses—so nearly human but also unearthly that Grandpa Walker said language couldn't quite describe it. And sometimes— or so Regine told the children—there was another sound too, a soft, musical voice that sang in time with the lions' chorus. Legend said too that once a white panther came to steal a settler's horse and rode away sitting upward on its back like a man.

Grandpa Walker's stories were written on the children's oldest memories. If they felt real, it was because they were as much a part of being a Brynn as were gray eyes and freckles.

That was why, when Mallory Brynn saw the white lion, she never doubted that it was real.

It was walking in long, languid strides down the halls of Mallory's school, but even the sight of a wild creature in school didn't make Mallory doubt that she was seeing something real. The animal was beautiful, a living snow statue, muscles bulging and rippling under a stainless soft pelt. It was beautiful except for the fact that the eyes in its great, triangular head were. . . somehow human.

The lion passed the alcove that led to the Little Theatre, where letters on an arch edged in green and white proclaimed, LOVE ART—FOR EVERYONE'S SAKE! It swung its great head side to side as if listening for a cue, then headed down the narrow corridor to the girls' locker room. There, in the dressing room, the cheerleaders' outfits were lined up as the coach insisted, their shoes, some as little as a fourth grader's, with pom-poms threaded onto the laces, were lined up below on a bench. Suddenly, with a flick of its paw, the lion reached up and swiped the last pair from the bench. And then, looking straight at Mallory with recognition and a sorrow she felt in her chest like a bruise, it pulled its lips back from its teeth and yowled like a soul in pain. Mallory heard the sound Grandpa Walker could never describe, the sound no Brynn had heard for two hundred years. And she knew it was meant for her.

Mallory screamed, jerking her body up in her bed, nearly knocking herself cold on the slanted roof of the attic bedroom she shared with Meredith.

Busy doing what she did best, staring into the mirror, Meredith froze. Then she went up like a rocket, screaming in stereo, a whole octave higher than her sister. It was pure Meredith super-drama, complete with a gasp and a threat: "Shut up! You almost gave me a heart attack!"

But something dark and old bloomed in Merry's chest too. She'd heard an echo of what had so frightened her sister, a terrible sound from the past. Merry and Mallory were mirror-image twins, as alike and unlike each other as two human beings could be. But since their birthday, nearly ten months before, and everything that came after that, they knew that whether she wanted to or not, Mallory could and would see into the future. Meredith could, and would, see into the past.

So whatever had screamed for Mallory wanted Merry too.

COMPLEX GIFTS

COMPLEX GIFTS

Pulling her comforter around her with a shiver, Mallory sat up and gave in to the slightest moment of ordinary sisterly irritability. Screaming was just so. . .second nature for Meredith: She screamed into her cell phone when one of her duh friends told her that her new crush had *actually looked directly at her* on the bus. She screamed when another of the band of genius girls Merry hung around with called to tell her that Uggs were on sale for 20 percent off at the Shoe Barn.

Both girls heard a muffled shout from their mother, Campbell. "What's going on? It's six in the morning!"

Merry called, "I'm sorry! I . . . I saw a mouse!"

"Smart move," Mallory whispered. "She'll be up here with a trap and peanut butter in fifteen seconds."

But Campbell only called back, "There's no mouse. It's too cold up here for mice!" Merry could hear their father Tim's muffled *oomph* as Campbell elbowed him in the side. "Tim, what did you use to insulate this side of the addition? Cotton balls?"

"Will everybody shut up?" Adam, the twins' younger brother, shouted. "I don't have to get up for half an hour!"

Mallory examined her ankles and wrists, rubbed her palms, pressed her cheekbones: They were as icy to the touch as if she'd just come off a ski slope, and it had nothing to do with the morning chill on the third story of the ancient house. Mallory felt as exhausted as though she had crawled into her bed after a long journey, climbing foot by foot over boulders, narrowly sliding away from each terrifying crevasse. She might as well not have slept at all.

Abruptly, she looked up at Merry and started to cry.

In a flash, Merry was on her knees, instantly forgetting the crisis that was ruining her life. She had been staring into the mirror for the past hour trying to figure out a way to camouflage the aftermath of an overnight miracle cure for zits given to her by Caitlin's older sister. "You put toothpaste on the pimples, and they will be gone by morning," Jackie told Meredith. Jackie was right: The zits were gone, replaced by huge, red, rough, dry patches. Meredith had gone from looking like a 'Before' ad for Oxy 10 to a page from a medical book on rare skin diseases.

But none of this mattered now, though, because Mallory was crying.

Mally cried about as often as she bought new clothes—once a year, if she was forced. The last time Merry had seen her twin cry was last summer, at the moment when their grandmother told them that their so-called "gift" would never go away. The terrifying, unwanted visions were to haunt their lives, forever—a fact like the fact that, although they were identical twins, they would never have the same birth year because Merry was born a minute before midnight on New Year's Eve and Mally a minute after. After the awful visions of last year, it was too much even for Mallory, who was so tough that when she gashed her knee on the soccer field, she did little more than wince. But just a few gentle words from their grandmother about the twins' legacy and Mally fell apart.

That was reason enough to interrupt Meredith's crisis.

"Ster," she asked, using their baby name for each other, "what's wrong? What happened?"

"I saw a cat." Mallory gulped, trying to swallow, hiccoughing and rubbing her eyes with the palms of her hands. "In a dream."

"You . . . saw a cat?" Merry gasped. "That's all?"

For this she had interrupted her perfectly justified breakdown over the fact that she was going to look like pond scum on the only day of her life she really *needed* to look good?

Today, the freshmen got the chance—their only chance—to try out for two spots on varsity . . . *in front of* the varsity cheerleaders, the senior football and basketball players, and the ultra-sexy girls from the pom-pom squad. Sometimes only one was chosen, and there were years when no one was good enough. Merry's stress over competing against her best friends (or worse, losing out to her best friends) had seeded a pimple plantation and prompted the extreme toothpaste cure.

Meredith didn't know whether to hug Mallory or push her off the bed. "You're crying because you dreamed you saw a cat? What's wrong with you?"

This was the part where Mallory would usually scowl and tell

Meredith to get out of her face: forget it, stuff a sock in it, let her alone, no big deal. But this time, pleading with her eyes, Mallory said, "It wasn't a cat like a *kitty cat*, Mer. It was a lion. A white mountain lion."

"A white. Mountain. Lion." Merry tossed her hair. "Please."

"It was in school. . . . "

"In school?"

"Yes, in school."

"Okay. This concerns me, why? I know! Not at all! Mallory, come on. Make sense."

Merry got up and went back to the mirror and the array of fifteen jars of foundation spread out on the twins' dressing table.

Then Mallory said softly, "Merry, it was in *school*, and in the girls' locker room, where the cheerleaders' outfits were. There was a row of shoes. . . ."

Merry sat down again.

If it had to do with the cheerleaders, it had to do with Merry. Along with Crystal Fish, she was JV co captain. Meredith tried to ignore the fact that what Mallory was saying was giving her the telltale swizzle of tiny electrical shocks along her arms that usually signaled a real vision. How could it be? The past visions were strange and fragmentary but had some slight connection with reality. A lion in the locker room? Mallory wouldn't have cried if an *actual* lion had walked into the locker room. She'd have climbed up onto a bench and started throwing field hockey sticks at it.

Carefully, Merry said, "Ster, it's weird and I know it scared you and it probably means something, but I don't think it means an escaped lion from the circus is going to get into our school and eat somebody. I don't think it's *that kind* of dream. And so now, I have to figure out how I can go to school today without looking like I have leprosy." More gently, she added, "Stop crying, Mallory. It was just . . . a symbol of your disgust for cheerleaders or something."

"Merry. I . . . knew her. It. The cat. Personally."

Merry was giving herself a headache standing up and sitting back down. She could feel a vein in her forehead start to throb.

"You knew the cat," she said. "Mallory, you sound like . . . me! You mean, the cat was a person in costume? Like a team mascot?"

"No, it wasn't that."

"You mean you knew the cat the way you know Sunny's puppy, Pippen? It was a regular cat in real life but giant-sized in your dream?"

When Mallory looked up, anger in her brimming eyes, Merry quickly recognized her mistake.

"No!" Mally said grimly.

Immediately Meredith said, "I'm sorry! Okay? I'm sorry!"

Mallory glared.

But the mere mention of Sunny Scavo's dog brought so much dark dust whirling back at them from the past—dust with, in its depths, half-visible things that neither wanted ever to see again. Everyone thought Sunny's dog had run away. But Mallory's vision of the dog, tortured by handsome David Jellico, had confirmed their suspicions about David's "cemetery" for so-called road-killed animals. And the truth about David's "cemetery" led to so much that the twins had to live with forever, but never tell. Kim Jellico, David's younger sister, had been Merry's best friend—at least until last spring. Merry had even had a schoolgirl crush on David.

But as their visions about David escalated into nightmares when he began stalking bigger game than cats and dogs, the twins were pushed into an elaborate game of cat-and-mouse. Scared out of their minds, they interrupted David's dates and showed up where they learned he would be, trying to make sure that David was never alone with a girl. And at last, he got wise. When they showed up in the muddy rubble of a new housing development where David had trapped some poor girl, no one knew what would have happened if Mallory hadn't found a nail gun left behind by one of the builders and used it to threaten David if he didn't stop.

But David didn't stop.

He stopped only when he fell to his death from Crying Woman Ridge, in a face-off with Merry, who he had cornered on the empty road up into the hills. As Merry stumbled with her bloody knees, some sight or sound had frightened David a moment before he would have shoved Merry to the rocks far below.

The whole mess was proof that what began the previous New Year's Eve was no passing mischief.

Still, they would never know everything that David had done in his hilltop garden. Yes, if some poor girl was buried up there, her parents should know. But David and Kim's mom, Bonnie Jellico, an operating-room nurse, had been their mother's closest friend forever. The twins couldn't turn to their own parents. With what proof? As it was, Campbell had them evaluated for everything from seizures to hormone imbalances. After the death, all they wanted was blessed ignorance. All they wanted was their own lives. As if they could ever have them again.

It started on their thirteenth birthday, when they were stuck at their uncle Kevin's, babysitting their brother and little cousins. At ten o'clock, a burst of fireworks—not firecrackers but the kind people saw at displays on the Fourth of July—went off outside. Suddenly, the roof was ablaze, exploding an ordinary dull evening into the deadliest night of their lives. Mallory was barely able to roll off the couch as the roof of the wraparound porch collapsed and the living room curtains swooped down in wings of flame. Confused by the darkness, choking on the smoke, she couldn't find her way. But with the kids herded to safety, Meredith crawled back into the black inferno of the living room. She knew only that unless she could find Mallory's hand, she would not be divided but erased. Risking her life to save her twin was risking her life to save her own.

And she had.

Somehow, Merry hauled her twin across the floor and out the door before both of them lost consciousness.

When they wakened in the hospital, they were grateful for their lives but alarmed that something between them had been severed forever. At first, they thought it might just be the shock of the fire and the rescue. But though the plum sunburn on Mallory's seared face faded, the scars on Merry's palms from her rescue mission were permanent. For the twins, those scars became a symbol of how they had "disconnected" after the fire.

Somehow, it burned away some essential part of their twin-ness.

If anyone had asked them before the fire, neither might have been able to put into words what that meant. It was beyond words—like the Northern Lights, a natural phenomenon that looked like magic except to people who saw it every day. Even their parents never questioned that Mallory and Meredith could talk to each other with their minds as readily as other people talked to each other with their voices. And though this remained, they still felt severed. They were shut out of each other's dreams, which used to flow between their sleeping minds, and could only find each other's thoughts with hard work, like picking locks. Their sight was turned outward, instead of trained on each other. The visions came in dreams, then in tiny fainting spells. But always, the visions came.

After David's death, they thought it was over until their grandmother, Gwenny Brynn, a twin who was the daughter of a twin and the granddaughter of a twin—all of whom had "the sight"—told them they would be this way forever.

But still, the girls only half believed her.

Until that Monday in fall when Mallory woke screaming, the other half kept hoping.

BACK TO THE FUTURE
BACK TO THE FUTURE

N ow, a huge gust of October wind threw the nearly bare branches of the huge maple outside the girls' window with the tapping of a hundred skeleton fingers, as if to remind them: It was back and waiting.

"There's nothing we can do but be ready," Mallory said to Merry.

"I don't think you ever get to be ready," Merry answered. "Last time, it took us totally by surprise. We didn't believe it. I think that's a pattern. If it was reasonable, and you had a warning and could figure it out, it wouldn't be psychicism."

"I don't think it's psychicism now," Mallory answered. "I don't know what to call it but that's not exactly a word. In our language."

"Well, psychic-ish," Merry said. "Visionism. Mediumism."

"You're right about one thing. There's no name for it. And it smacks you right across the shoulder blades just when you think you've got a big lead on it."

They both thought of the long, clean, green, and vanished summer.

The hassles of being the pre-clairvoyant Brynn twins—the teasing for being both the smallest *and* the youngest kids in their grade, the odd looks Mallory got from a teacher when she couldn't for the life of her remember even the *name* of the French national anthem and then, after a mental call for help to Merry, suddenly sang out the first line with perfect enunciation—it all seemed so sweet and far away.

"It really was great compared to now," Mallory said, agreeing with an observation Meredith hadn't spoken—at least not aloud. "I'd give my left molar to change it back."

"You and me both," Merry said.

"You know what Mom says: If wishes were horses . . . "

". . . Everybody would have one," Merry finished for her.

"No. It's: If wishes were horses, beggars would ride!" Mally said impatiently. "It means that everyone wishes for things that they can't have, and if wishes came true, even poor people would be like everyone else."

"But they'd still want horses."

Mallory sighed. "Oh, Merry, you'll never change." She thought, *I'd never have believed how comforting that would be.* For an instant, Mallory cherished how Merry would always be the embodiment of her nickname—a buoyant performer who would rather talk to the Animal Channel than be quiet.

And Merry, who usually despaired of Mallory, an antisocial lump who liked only soccer and soap operas, suddenly couldn't imagine a world without Mallory, who thought she looked just great in her mesh gym shorts two sizes too big.

Merry's hair still parted on the right and Mally's on the left. Merry still wrote with her right hand and Mallory with her left. They still had identical sprinkles of cinnamon freckles across their noses. They still each weighed ninety pounds and stood 4'11 ¼" tall.

No one except the twins would have seen them as different from before or different from each other.

No one could have grasped just how miserable it was to again have to face the fact that they were independent beings with independent psychic powers.

"I started to think it was over too," Merry began. "And not because everything's orange Jell-O to me, like you keep saying to everyone. I take it as seriously as you do."

"It's just that you haven't had a dream like the old ones yet, and you'll know when you do," Mally said darkly.

"I'm not stupid, Mallory. They look different."

Mallory perked up. "They do to you too? Is it like . . . I don't know . . . they're like movies. Like a real film instead of a soap opera?"

"They're deeper," Meredith agreed, but added, "I wish we didn't know that."

"I wish someone besides Grandma knew that we did," Mallory admitted. "Someone . . . normal. Not that Grandma's not normal."

"I know what you mean. Someone like . . . us."

"Our age," Mally said, and thought for a moment how, last winter, she'd begun to confide in one of her older teammates on the Eighty-Niners, Eden Cardinal. Eden seemed to understand—to more than understand, really. But Mallory stopped short of telling the whole truth. What if Eden really knew? She'd run. She'd think Mallory was a head case . . . or worse. It was too much to risk. Eden was a junior, a popular junior, and the closest thing Mallory had to an actual girl friend. She went out of her way to call Mallory, to come over and force her to come out for a cup of coffee at Latte Java—even after both twins withdrew into a closed society of two following David's death. Mallory was grateful. But if regular people knew the real story . . . what if they thought that she and her sister were involved in David's gruesome games? No, no, no. Having secrets was horrible. Being alone with them was horrible. The only worse thing would be other people knowing.

"You're right," Merry said. "They'd just talk about us later."

"I didn't say that. Did you *hear* me?"

"No, it was honest-to-God just a hunch," Merry admitted. Without meaning to, for a moment, both of them grinned.

"Drew doesn't," Mally said. "He knows and he doesn't talk about us."

"Drew only knows the outlines," Merry pointed out.

Drew Vaughn, their neighbor, had known the twins since they were born. Even the terrors of the past ten months hadn't scared him off. In fact, he'd lost his job because of the number of times during the David crisis that he had run off to answer the twins' strange requests or panicky phone calls. Because he was steadfast, they got to keep their lives, at least from the outside. Merry's friends could still be counted on to swear friendship forever or war to the end—and you could be sure that the vows would last the entire weekend. Big mouths on the team made snide remarks about Mally being so short, she could run through the legs of the defenders, until she brought the Eighty-Niners another trophy. Their mother was a stickler, their brother infuriating, their father happily flaky.

What the twins had become might be as big and mysterious as a dark galaxy, but it could never consume their small, bright, ordinary, annoying, and beloved world.

And now, they would hold on to that world like a rope in a high wind.

THE END OF INNOCENCE

THE END OF INNOCENCE

B y the time Mallory had showered away her tears and Merry had applied enough makeup to resemble a Kabuki dancer, both girls were composed enough to race downstairs, grab a bagel, and jump into Drew's car. Merry planned her own dash with care. Although she normally wouldn't have been caught dead in a hoodie, she borrowed one of her sister's biggest ones to slip out under cover before her mother noticed how peculiar she looked.

"You're postponing the inevitable," Mallory told her.

"Exactly," her twin agreed.

Merry's mother was usually halfway ready to be in a bad mood just from having twins who were almost fourteen and an eleven-year-old son. She was freshly frazzled by a new full-time job as the chief emergency room nurse at Ridgeline Memorial. It was a crushing schedule with more chaos than Campbell liked. Sleep had become her sacrament, and the twins had awakened her by yelling.

So Merry was already on thin ice when, just two strides from the door, she heard her mother say, "Meredith. What happened to your face?"

Merry said, "I'm . . . I'm trying a new makeup."

"You look like you escaped from the mummy diorama at the Natural History Museum."

"If I take it off, it'll be worse."

Campbell lowered her newspaper. "I, ah, doubt that."

Meredith grabbed a clean washcloth, ran it under the tap, and dabbed at a small place on her forehead. She turned to face her mom. Campbell stood up. "Meredith!"

"I wanted my skin to be clear for tryouts!" Merry pleaded.

"So you touched it up with a blowtorch?" her mom asked, as skeevy little Adam started making noises like the sound of bacon frying.

Reluctantly, Merry explained the toothpaste cure.

"Brilliant," Campbell said. "That's brilliant, Meredith. Could I have a minute's peace? Well. Let's get some heavy-duty moisturizer on it. And I'll ask a dermatologist if there's something I can bring at noon." She began dabbing judiciously at Meredith's temples. "It's worse up here. You'll be lucky if this clears up by Christmas!"

"That's three months!"

"I was exaggerating," said Campbell. "But winter's clearly coming early if mice are coming in."

The house did have an unseasonable chill for so early in October. Tim banned heat until Halloween. For a few weeks, they'd have to get out the sweaters with the big weird flowers and farm animals on them, the ones knitted by Grandma Gwenny—which no one ever wore anywhere outside except to Grandma's or places like church, where no one cared if you looked like you were wearing the wrapping paper for a fruitcake.

"Mom, you're an angel," Merry said fervently, hugging Campbell impulsively.

"Everyone says so," Campbell replied, giving Merry a shoulder squeeze when her usual behavior would have been to wrap her daughter in an octopus grip. She turned back to her newspaper, and, with just the wisp of a puzzled glance, Meredith ran out the door. Mallory was slipping into the front seat and withdrawing into the tent of her own hoodie.

"What's up, Brynn?" Drew asked. He meant Mallory, who was truly his buddy and who wouldn't have answered if he'd called her by anything but her last name.

"Didn't sleep much," Mallory said. "Didn't go for my run, so I'm not awake. *And* I don't feel like talking."

"What else?"

"If I wanted to tell you why I'm not talking, then I'd be talking. Which I'm not."

"Meow!" Drew said.

Merry spoke up, "That reminds me. I had this idea about the lion. . . ."

"Laybite!" Mallory cautioned her, using their old twin-language for "Stop it!" She said again, so quietly Drew didn't hear, "Laybite, shosi-on-up-on."

"Excuse me for thinking!" Merry snapped.

"Don't bother," Mallory told Merry. "I'll let it pass because you don't do it much."

"Lions and tigers and bears, oh my," Drew teased them. "Maybe you're wearing animal prints to Homecoming. Isn't that what they call them? My mom says those are in this year." Merry smirked. No one ever saw Mrs. Vaughn's clothes because, although Drew's sisters were in college, their mom still put on an apron the size of a pup tent and baked five loaves of bread and five dozen cookies a week. She must leave them on people's porches after dark, the way Aunt Kate did with bags of carrots and zucchini. "Aren't dresses on the tiny minds of females this time of year?"

"In your dreams," Mally said. "Which is to say, not mine."

"Oh well," Drew said, cranking up one of the ancient rock CDs in his collection. "Stop praying. I've already got a date."

Mally sighed. "I should warn her you have athlete's foot."

"Don't try to fool me, Brynn. I know you're speechless."

"That would be because I'm sleeping. I can get in ten good minutes before school. It's freezing in here." As if it heard her, the wind obligingly blew a bushel of dry leaves through the passenger-side window. Mallory sat up to spit out a mouthful. "Ugh! I just used Pearl Strips on my teeth." Both of them stared at her, Drew nearly taking out his own mailbox. "Well, don't look like I said I had a hair transplant! I do like my teeth to be nice!"

"Pearl Strips?" Meredith gasped. "You just started flossing last year!"

This is Monday to the tenth power, Mallory thought.

"It doesn't close," Drew apologized. "The window fell down

into the well that day I bulldozed the housing development playing mortal combat with David Jellico."

"Which we jokingly refer to as the first time he tried to kill me and my sister," Mally snapped.

"Forgive me for wrecking my car to stop him! How quickly we forget the knight in shining armor!"

"Hardly shining . . ." Mally said, stifling a yawn. Drew's green Toyota was now verifiably two-tone, rust-over-emerald.

"Jeez, Brynn! You're snarky even for you. What's eating you this morning?" Drew asked, leaning across Mallory to turn up the volume on the CD player. As quickly as he did, Merry slipped out and back into her seat belt in order to turn it back down.

"You don't have to blast that thing!" Merry shouted. "I am a human being too, you know. You can talk to me."

"Okay," Drew said, "I'm loving the mask."

Blushing, although no one could tell, Merry said, "It's a skin treatment." Merry had just applied a new layer of makeup over the moisturizer.

"Hope it works," Drew said. "I mean that sincerely."

They passed Tony Arno, who ran the five miles to school in miniscule shorts until the temperatures hit the single digits—to the disgust of all the guys and the rapture of the girls—and somehow never stank the rest of the day. "Hi, Tony!" Merry called out the window, smacking heads with her sister, who appeared not to waken. "He's so cute. He could have any girl."

"Yes, he's very cute," Drew agreed with a sigh. "Especially the Speedo."

"You're just jealous. I heard he likes Neely," Meredith went on. She began to chatter about Neely Chaplin, the new girl from Chicago, and Merry and Caitlin's only real rival for the second spot on varsity. Meredith didn't want to brag, she said, but she basically considered her own spot assured. Her tumbling alone would nail it.

"I may have ignored this before," Drew said. "Ten times at least, but not because it isn't fascinating."

"Drew, you know flyers are the hardest to find."

"Absolutely. I have a hard time finding *you* if your dad forgets to cut the grass. Or forgets to get me to cut it."

The last few blocks were crowded with bikers and, as they neared the school, the smokers, who gathered around the fire hydrant at the required fifty feet from the school entrance, exactly opposite the picture window of the principal's office.

By that point, Meredith had wound herself up so tightly on the subject of tryouts that she was like a mechanized toy, practically bouncing in the seat; she couldn't have stopped if Drew had burst into flames. As he turned into the lot, Merry went on, "You know, Drew, small can be weak. And you can be a flyer and still be a lousy tumbler. But if you're strong, you can be too big to get thrown. I can do both. That's why Crystal isn't all-around. Imagine trying to lift Crystal Fish on one shoulder."

"I actually imagine that quite a bit," Drew said. Crystal was totally gorgeous, all five feet, eight inches of her, with twisty blond hair that hung to her hips and legs that the boys at Ridgeline seemed to consider some kind of local resource, like a silver mine.

"Don't be such a stereotype. Guys revolt around Crystal like planets around the sun," Merry said. "It's absurd."

"They revolve, you mean," Drew said gently.

"They revolt around you," Mallory said, waking up.

"It's true. I haven't had a serious relationship in six months," Merry said. "Am I doing something wrong?"

"Not that I can see. Guys love women who never close their cell phones," Drew said. "It gives them their space."

But Merry was deep in conversation on the phone with Alli, who was repeating her comments to Caitlin, and waving to Erika. The cheerleaders approached the car and absorbed Meredith as she hopped out of the backseat, as if they were first graders playing amoeba tag.

"You want to get out here too, Brynn?" Drew asked gently. From within her hoodie, Mallory shook her head, and Drew headed for his usual parking space behind the field house.

The first bell howled like a tornado siren.

GOLDEN EYES

For Merry, ten minutes between bells were a lifetime of gossip opportunities. She ran with Alli and Caitlin, Erika and Crystal falling into rank like soldiers, to "their" table in the Commons. It seemed an eternity since the last time they'd seen one another, nearly forty-eight hours ago.

Meanwhile, still in the parking lot, startled by the sound of the bell, Mallory almost hopped out before Drew finished parking. Then she flopped back against the seat.

Why bother?

Something was wrong. She didn't know what.

Drew looked at her with concern.

"Brynn, you want me to walk you in? What's going on?"

"Nothing really, Drewsky. I'm sorry I was a jerk this morning."

"Don't change for me, Brynn," Drew said with a laugh. "You're a jerk every morning." He tried again. "Brynn? You know you can't hide from me. You have the look on your face that freaks me out. With good reason, I might add. I fear that look. It usually involves some kind of damage for me." He pulled the top of her hoodie down over her eyes.

"I was only teasing before, Drew," Mallory said softly. "I hope you have a great Homecoming. Who're you going with?"

"Pam Door."

"Captain of the cheerleaders and a senior! You big stud!" Mally said.

Drew almost said he was settling for Pam Door because he couldn't have the girl next door, but had long ago made the choice to keep Mallory his buddy instead of giving in to the crush he'd felt for years. But as they began to go their separate ways, she looked so small and vulnerable in his old black hoodie. Something was wrong, he thought, with a quick twist of his gut. She hadn't even tried to slug him when he jerked her hood down over her eyes.

Mallory could feel herself tuning Drew out as she headed for the main entrance. She could barely muster a wave. Drew was watching her as though she had sprouted tentacles from the crown of her shiny cap of black hair. But she didn't look back. The unease dripped down her neck like cold droplets. She hadn't warmed up since she'd opened her eyes. What was it? Mallory hadn't seen anything, unless you counted a big white cat knocking over some cheerleading shoes.

Not like David. Not like any of that. Dragging her feet, she walked slowly toward the big glass doors of C building.

Just as she took her first step inside, someone grabbed the back of her sweatshirt. Turning sharply, she found herself face-to-face with Eden Cardinal, whose gleaming hair was brushed long and loose today, blue-black in the sun.

"What's up, Shortie?" she asked Mallory. "Are you some kind of spy for elves?" Mallory glanced down, then looked up at Eden and grinned. She was wearing black from the top of her head to the tips of her Converse high-tops. She hadn't noticed.

"Yes," she said. "I'm undercover to report girls whose butts are hanging below their skirts. That's my eye level." Eden laughed and grabbed Mallory's arm. It still amazed Mally that a junior like Eden, who couldn't have possibly answered the number of "hellos" directed her way as she walked down the hall, didn't brush off Mallory's lowly freshman self like dandruff. Mally never called Eden to suggest they do something. She wouldn't have dared. But when Eden called her, she was always up for anything, even running errands. So grateful was she to see Eden and comforted by her assured presence, Mallory almost opened her mouth to spill her worries.

But Eden spoke first.

"Mal," she said. "There's something I have to tell you. I mean ask you. I mean find out from you." Eden turned all giggly and bubbly, in a way she never was, almost like Merry's merry band of nits. What was that about? "Your dad owns Domino Sports and I need . . . sort of a sporting good."

They slipped into a corner of the glassed-in Commons. *Exactly where I saw the lion,* she thought with that same cold creep of anxiety. Eden popped two dollars in change into the coffee machine and handed Mallory a steaming cup of hot chocolate before grabbing one of her own. Mally finally remembered her manners and noticed that the paper cup was hot as a live coal. "Thanks! Ow!" she said. "Yikes. My hand is so cold I didn't realize I was getting second-degree burns."

"I know! It's freezing today," Eden said. "I wore gloves!"

"And plus, I'm brain-dead today. I slept just awful-awful. Now, what were you saying? What's a sort-of sporting good?"

They were interrupted briefly to watch Mr. Yee forcibly untangle Trevor Solwyn and her boyfriend, who were making out against the pillar way too ferociously for 8:06 A.M.

Eden said, "I know your dad's fall sale is coming up, and I wondered if he had any double sleeping bags."

"Sure. He keeps a couple of them, mostly for wedding presents for people who are going camping on their honeymoon. Which I think is sort of a contradiction in terms, don't you? If I ever get married, it's a big hotel in Maui or nothing."

Mally and Eden slipped into the crowds making their way out of the Commons. Both of them had math first hour—Eden in Pre-Calc across the hall from Mally in Geometry.

"I think it would be incredibly romantic, being in a sleeping bag in the wilderness with the man you loved, like being inside each other's skin or something," Eden said.

"Ugh! I might be a jock but I hate sleeping on the ground! I hate it at our family's camp when we have outdoor night."

"I love the stars," Eden said.

"So are you running away to get married?" Mallory teased

and was horrified when Eden's face paled under its perpetual rosy gold.

"Uh, no. Not really . . . I . . . well, it's a gift. For a friend. A guy."

Mally asked, "Is it someone you like, I mean . . . like?"

"Yes."

"And you're giving him a wedding present?"

"It's for him and me. When we meet." To Mallory's wide-eyed look, Eden said, "Not like that! Not that it would be bad. He's twenty-one! I'm almost eighteen! But it's not like that. We just have to meet, well, secretly."

"Because he's older?"

"Partly. Look, forget it. I shouldn't have brought it up."

"Eden!" Mallory said. "I'm just worried because . . . I'm just scared for you."

"Why?" Eden asked quickly.

"Never mind. It's just this stupid feeling. What color sleeping bag?"

Eden looked down at her shoes. "Well, red is his favorite."

"Okay!" Mally said, throwing her book bag into her locker as the second bell pealed. "I'll check this weekend when I go in to . . ." Before she could close her locker door, Mallory staggered and stumbled. For an instant, Eden seemed to shrink to a dot the size of a pencil point. Mallory woke sitting on the ground, with Eden crouched in front of her.

"Mally? Mallory?" Eden said, suddenly her normal size again, her voice as loud as a crowded gym during a basketball game.

Mallory covered her ears. "How long have I been on the floor?"

"Just a few seconds," Eden said. "What happened?"

Mallory thought how impossible it would be for her to explain. She had flashed on a young man lying wrapped in a huge red sleeping bag. And it was definitely . . . James. Mallory had seen James before. On the cold, miserable day when she confided in Eden about their visions, she'd "wake-dreamed" James walking along, whistling, in the fading light, under the greedy gaze of a mountain lion perched on an outcropping of granite.

"It's James," Mallory said. "I saw him last year, remember? I told you how dangerous the lion was to the guy on the hike, and you tried to brush it off. That's who the sleeping bag is for."

"Yes," said Eden.

"But he really is in danger! You said it wasn't like it seemed."

"It isn't."

"I saw it, Edie!"

"You don't know what you saw. It's like . . . you and me being friends. You think I met you when you came on the Eighty-Niners. But I knew you before then. I saw you around when you were little. You're in my pattern, written on the star blanket."

"What?"

"The sky. The star blanket," Eden said softly, her old, calm self again, not the angry, fierce, unfamiliar girl of just moments ago. "It's all up there, what's supposed to happen to people, and who they're supposed to be with."

"I don't understand," Mally said.

"You don't have to," Eden told her gently.

Mallory looked into Eden's big dark eyes and thought she saw a fleck of gold glimmering there, amid the velvet brown. Golden eyes.

What?

Shaking Eden's hand off, Mallory turned and hurried down the hall, dodging groups of kids to break into a jog, then a run, not looking back even when she heard Eden call her name. Forget math class. She'd fake a sinus headache and chill out in the nurse's office. Backtracking, she passed the door of the little theater and felt waves of menace furl out of the double doors. She stopped to catch a breath.

At that moment, Mallory knew for certain that no one was going to get up on that stage after school and kick and flip and punch out their little fists to "Ridgeline, So Fine!" or "Bring It Home!" Her sister, Merry, didn't have to worry. No one would notice her lacquered face. There would be no tryouts today.

She had no idea why.

But Eden . . . there was something wrong, something that made Mallory's skin go tight and cold—as it had when the mountain lion shrieked.

THE CHEER NOT SPOKEN

THE CHEER NOT SPOKEN

Later that morning, Merry was in history class when the P.A. system boomed, "Meredith Brynn. Please report to the office." Merry tried to slink out along the wall, but heard Neely, the new girl, whispering with Erika. One of them said, "Nice look, Mer!"

Merry wished a chute to the core of the earth would open and she could just allow herself to drop into nothingness.

Campbell was waiting with a small brown bag. Together, they slipped into the washroom and Meredith washed her face. Then Campbell dabbed on the stuff she'd brought, a drop at a time from the tube. Scared to open her eyes, Merry turned toward the mirror. The concealer really did work! She no longer looked like someone who'd died earlier in the day from smallpox. Merry hugged her mother. "You saved my future!"

Campbell said, "This stuff is thicker than the department store kind. And it's waterproof, which I thought would be good if you got sweaty. It's for covering up, well, scars and stuff like that."

Merry noticed her mother trying to slip the box into the trash and grabbed it. The brand was called AfterLife.

AfterLife? Meredith looked at the back. "Creating a memory picture of the loved one," it said. In a quivery voice, Merry asked, "What is this? Did you bring me . . . undertaker cosmetics?"

Campbell shrugged. "Maggie Lonergran was in the ER for a broken toe. She sent her son Luke back to grab a tube for you. Take it or leave it, Meredith! You're not going to cover up that mess with a little powder." Lonergran's was the only funeral parlor in Deptford. Meredith had been there exactly once, one of the worst days of her life, for David Jellico's funeral.

"But ick, Mom!"

"Merry, it's not recycled!" Campbell said sharply. Campbell was *such* a crab lately.

"I'm sorry," Merry said. "I was just thinking about . . ."

"I know, honey. Look, let's make a deal. We won't tell Adam so he can't get in your face about it, and everything will be all right, okay?" Merry noticed new lines of weariness on Campbell's face: The new job was clearly too much for her. She didn't even have time to run anymore, and she was getting a potbelly. Merry had overheard Campbell tell their father that if they didn't need the extra money, they could stuff combat pay. She decided to take it easy on her mom, who had done her best.

Merry put on some light foundation and blush over the concealer and added just a little gray eye shadow and more mascara. This amounted to about 75 percent more makeup than Merry ever wore except for a cheer competition.

"You still don't look like you," Campbell said.

"But I look like a person," Merry said.

Later, in the cafeteria, Merry pulled her sister aside.

"I look pretty normal," Meredith said. "Don't I, Mal?"

"You never look normal," Mally answered, obviously back to her old self.

Merry persisted. "Come on! You're not even looking!"

"I don't have to. Bug off, Mer. I have bigger stuff on my mind."

"I'm serious," Merry said.

"So am I," Mallory answered. "I have a quiz next hour."

"That's not what you meant."

"No, it isn't." Mallory glanced up, a half-gnawed pita in one hand, and stuck a pencil behind her ear. "It's way more than that. But I have to figure it out. You do look . . . um, better. I'm sorry. I can't concentrate."

Meredith decided she *did* look normal. What she didn't look was natural.

She looked the way Danielle Sibelius looked on an ordinary day—as though she were made up for Halloween or the red carpet outside the MTV music video awards. Danielle Sibelius wore skirts so short that Merry and Mallory's father would have made the twins wear them over jeans. Danielle wore double layers of false eyelashes. If she was honest with herself, Merry didn't even look as *good* as Danielle Sibelius because makeup on Meredith made her look a little sinister—given her pint size—like a sort of old-time *Bride of Chuckie* doll.

It *was* almost Halloween.

"I'll find Drew and ask him," Merry said, turning back to Mallory. "He'll tell me honestly."

"What are you going to do about it when he does?" Mally asked. "Anyhow, it doesn't even matter, Mer."

"It doesn't matter? Because it's my tryouts and not yours? Because I don't have to fall in the dirt and slap other girls on the butt and make fart noises? Because I'm as good as you, but I get to be a girl too instead of pretending to be a boy with boobs? All you do is disrespect my sport!" Mallory snorted, which only made Merry madder. "That so stinks! Do you even think it's a sport? If you don't, do this, okay?" Meredith held her leg straight out in front of her, at hip height, for twenty seconds. "Do it, Mallory. Come on." Merry's leg was granite-steady. "Come on, Mal."

"Okay, I admit you're an Olympic leg holder."

"Admit that you don't have that kind of leg strength."

"I can't admit I don't because I do."

Mally was trying her best—she had to act like herself instead of the little simpy-wimp she'd been this morning—but even sarcasm was an effort. For a moment, Mally wished that she and Drew still had the basket on the fishing wire they used to pass notes back and forth between their open windows.

That would mean they would still be kids. Which would be fine with her.

Now, telling all to Drew was getting tricky: He might have known her since she was a baby, but Mallory could tell that he now considered her a babe. She didn't want to encourage that.

Or maybe she did.

No! Drew was like a brother!

Still, he was getting to be kind of cute.

Everything was turning upside down!

For the rest of the day, she wandered from class to class, half-aware. She wished she'd held the thermometer that Mrs. Avis put in her mouth against the light for a couple of seconds and been sent home with a fever.

At last, she did what you do when something is driving you crazy: She faced it. In her study period, Mallory tried to analyze her dream.

Mally now suspected that what David saw when he lunged for Merry was . . . a pale cat. A cougar. A mountain lion. A panther. All the names people used once, and still used, for one kind of animal. Back then, Meredith had described seeing just a shape, a long low white shape—and it wasn't the translucent figure of a white-haired lady with a kind face who leaned over her after she fell. Grandma Gwenny assured them that the little old lady was an ancestor, a Massenger woman, perhaps the kindly ghost of Grandma's own mother. At her own wish, Grandma Gwenny's mother had been buried not in the town cemetery but high on the ridges where she loved to walk at the end of a long day of cleaning other people's houses. Once a month, sometimes with the girls, Gwenny tended the two white rosebushes she'd planted near the modest copper plate in the ground that showed where her mother lay. Only last year had she told the girls that one of the rosebushes was meant to symbolize Gwenny's own twin, Vera, who'd drowned as a child. Gwenny regretted that she had never moved Vera's poor little wooden box up into the hills near the family camp, where she could sleep beside her mother. Grandma was a halfway decent Catholic, not a fanatic like some of her siblings were. But she also thought that anywhere love abided was holy ground.

So if Merry—and David—had seen not a woman but a cougar, was it too a spirit? Or some crazy sign? Cougars were extinct in the east, and if one had wandered down from Canada, it had wandered a long, long way. Did it hate men, which would have accounted for Mallory seeing it staring down so hungrily on the boy Eden loved? Was it a zoo animal, which would account for its exotic coloration?

During study hall, she slipped into the library and typed in "Cat Mythology."

Bast, a god in cat form, was one of the top guns in the Egyptian pantheon. Many ancient religions considered cats spirit guides for humans, wise but unable to reveal their wisdom because they could not speak. Was this what the mountain lion meant? And why was she seeing it, now that David was gone? Why had it appeared in their school, when clearly no real animal had been there? Was it still after Eden's boyfriend? Or was it after Eden?

She was ashamed that she'd run away from Edie.

How could her visions be so at odds with what she felt inside?

David had been model-handsome and a monster. But long before the visions, Mallory sensed something way off base about David. Eden wasn't like David. Her heart told her Eden was caring and good.

Grandma had told them that "the gift" came from above, that it was meant for them to use for good, that it was granted the twins for a reason that only the saints knew. She had to do this: She accepted that it was her destiny. Grandma Gwenny told her that the gift went down among the Massenger women like a gene for hair color (or a disease, Mally thought!).

The last bell rang. Mally looked up toward the sky. The star blanket.

She didn't realize until later that her lips had moved and hoped everyone who saw her thought she was using an earpiece for her cell, as she addressed the giver of the damned gift.

She said, "If this really is what my grandmother believes it is, and you want us to fight for the right or whatever, can I please at least have some rules?"

That was when she heard the scream.

SPLIT DIVISION

C rystal Fish went on screaming all the way into the ambulance from the pain of torn ligaments that would need surgery and months of physical therapy. Her hope of making varsity as a sophomore was shot.

The tryouts were postponed until the second week in November. Mallory felt sorry for Crystal. Hitting the floor in Chinese splits when it was only possible for you to get there after a half-hour warm-up must have been killer.

"Someone put tape on her shoes," Merry told Mallory after the ambulance left. They sat down in the cafeteria to wait for Drew to be finished with cross-country.

"But why?" Mallory asked.

"It's a cheat. People used to do it to slide better, but it's illegal because, obviously, it makes you go too fast. This can happen to someone even if she knows the tape is there."

"Maybe she put it there herself," Mally suggested, opening her math book.

"Impossible. Crystal is a total stickler for stuff like that. And plus, she can do horizontal splits anyhow. She can do regular splits against a wall if she's warmed up."

"Well," Mallory said, lowering her voice, although the twins were alone in the Commons. "I saw the shoes. This must have something to do with . . . you know." She made her hands into small claws.

"How do you know you saw it flip over Crystal's shoes?" Merry asked, equally quietly. "They could have been anyone's. They could have been mine."

"You don't get to see stuff that's about yourself."

"I'm not yourself."

"I know but kind of . . . I heard you call me on the ridge when you were up there and David . . ."

"But I called you. That's different," Merry said. She began to gnaw her pencil. "I think."

"Well, nobody got a fractured skull at least," Mallory said.

It was one less thing to worry about. And for that day and for days to come, they simply didn't talk about it.

Mallory decided to use the time between alerts from the universe to take care of herself. She settled down at practice the next afternoon for the first time in a week.

And she had never looked so good, turning from offense to defense on a dime, as the great midfielders should. Her only sadness was the emptiness left by losing Eden's friendship. Mally hadn't realized just how much she counted on the time she spent with

Eden. Elegant, slender, and tough, Eden still performed on the field like a pro—the queen of defense, knocking shots away with her knees or her chest as if she wore armor instead of kneepads. But she looked right through Mallory. It broke Mally's heart.

Meanwhile, in Crystal's absence, Merry led practice alone for the rest of the week. She led it with a vengeance, to prove to herself that she was a real athlete as much as her jock sister.

"Okay, let's harden up those inner thighs," she said. "Hands on the floor. V-position. Wider. No wobbles. Now, raise and lower. Raise and lower. And raise. I'll count it. One. Two."

"Can you count any slower?" Alli yelled. "It's ten seconds by the clock and you're up to three."

"Let's hold to twenty," Merry said impassively.

"Remember when we were little and my brother almost knocked your teeth out with his lacrosse bat?" Caitlin called. "What went wrong there?"

"Does this mean you want to hold for a count of fifty?" Merry asked and then finally, as the girls groaned in relief, said, "Okay, let's stretch. Nose down over your right knee. Lift up from the hips and lean over. And over. Now, deep in the middle. And now we're ready to lift and go for thirty."

Girls were screaming by the end of the second series. When they were finished practicing the floor cheers, the stunting and their dance, Merry announced a cool-down jog, twice around the perimeter of the school, or a distance of two miles. Alli literally punched her on the arm. Merry said, "Get going, Lard." Alli had hips that were a little rounder than everyone else's. Though she was in no way fat, she acted like she was size 20.

"Who're you calling Lard, Squirt?" Alli snapped, breaking into laughter.

The only one who didn't object to anything and did everything just a little better and a little longer than Merry did was Neely Chaplin. Merry asked for twenty push-ups; Neely did thirty. Merry did a double back across the floor. Neely did a triple and ended with a round-off. She dusted off her hands and said, "Bring it, Merry."

What a little queenie!

What was Neely trying to prove, other than that she was the most insufferable rich kid to ever attend Ridgeline High? And that wasn't easy, considering Trevor Solwyn and Gina DeGloria and a few others who lived over in Haven Hills, a "golf-course community," a big glop of one-acre houses on one-acre yards. (Neely's was a two-acre house on a *three-acre* yard.) They acted so all-that, it made the regular townies sick.

And now the gung-ho Neely made Merry wonder. Could she be the person with the secret stash of tape? Neely acted so above all the rest of them, with her gourmet low-cal lunches and the long dark Lincoln Continental that picked her up from school every day. Everyone made such a big fuss over her, so Merry decided to make an art form of ignoring Neely. When Neely did triple backs to a round-off and front over for warm-ups, Merry concentrated on making sure there were no spaces between the maps. When she did full splits at the place in the dance where everyone was required to do a half, Merry said softly, "Let's all be synchronized, guys. Let's make it pretty."

And it worked.

One day, when Merry was carefully ignoring her, twisting tiny braids into the front of her black bob and pinning each one down— you never knew who might come to your sister's fall soccer game— Neely turned and said, "I asked Caitlin and Alli if they wanted to sleep over Friday, and I wanted to ask you too."

Merry waited a full count of three. Slow.

Then she said, "Three's company, right?"

She didn't need Neely's charity invitation. Alli's and Caitlin's moms didn't work. Alli's father owned two health clubs in Deptford. Neely probably saw them as her equals.

But Neely just smiled and said, "Come on! Four is more gossip. Don't be so stuck up."

"Me?" Merry began to laugh. She said, "Well, okay. But I have to go see Crystal. She had surgery yesterday."

"Come after. Poor Crystal. I'd go see her too, if I knew her better. Although I have to admit she's a little all-that with the movie-star twisty hair. I'm intimidated."

Meredith laughed again. Neely intimidated? For Meredith, heaven would be a place where she could flip through the *Bliss* catalog and mark every product she wanted. How could someone who ordered her clothes from boutiques in, like, Miami, as Alli said Neely did, and who lived in a house with eight bedrooms and two pools want . . . anything on earth?

Merry would look back later and think she was some fabulous psychic: She would have to wait a long time to learn the answer, and she would never have guessed it.

ALL FALL DOWN
ALL FALL DOWN

A nurse made the twins wait in the corridor while Crystal took her pain medication.

"She's afraid we'll see what kind of pills they are," Merry whispered. "Like we couldn't be addicts if we wanted to."

"That's not funny," Mallory said. "Some kids whose mothers are nurses really are like that. This is just a privacy thing for Crystal."

"Mallory, could you *be* more of a stick?" Merry griped.

The room they finally walked into looked like a combination of a florist's shop and a pep rally. There were green-and-white streamers and vases of carnations and single-stemmed roses everywhere. And there was a big heart arrangement with real white roses and green ribbons signed by Neely Chaplin.

As they walked in, Mallory whispered to her sister, "Seeleye."

"She did not," Merry said automatically.

In twin language, it meant something like "It's a lie" or "She's a fake." Mallory thought that Neely was probably the one responsible for Crystal's injury. But Merry wasn't sure. Neely *had* worn a different outfit for thirty school days straight at the beginning of the year—Merry had counted. But being rich didn't make you a secret assassin. Being a snot didn't make you a schemer who was so ruthless she'd do anything.

It didn't hurt, though.

"Who did not what?" Crystal asked. She opened the box of chocolates the twins brought and started poking the bottoms, looking for caramel—which she hated. She barely acknowledged them with a thank-you.

Merry said, "Oh, nothing. Mallory's just on about something! Oh, Crystal. This is horrible! You must be so uncomfortable and sad too!"

"I can take a lot of pain," Crystal said, with a dark look at Mallory. Obviously, Merry had told everybody cheerleaders weren't real athletes, and now they all hated Mallory's guts even more than usual. "All cheerleaders live with pain. But this is unbelievable. The ligaments were shredded like string cheese. I *heard* them go *sprong*. And like, why? Why did this happen to me?"

"It's so unfair, I know," Merry said.

"It's not like I would be above illegal," Crystal said casually. "When there's something I want, I'll do anything. Except hurt somebody. That's where I draw the line. And there's nothing they could have asked that I couldn't do." Crystal knew exactly how beautiful and flexible she was. She had a grudge against Coach for giving her less floor time than the flyers and was so into herself that she would never have risked anything that would give her an inch-long scar and keep her from working out every day. *Crystal could have been the chosen one,* Merry thought. She certainly looked older than a freshman and had a real body. There *was* the sex appeal factor.

Standing on the other end of the room, Mallory thought, *Typical cheerleader.* She concentrated deliberately to make sure her sister heard. Meredith did and, as quick as a snake would, stuck out her tongue.

"The best I can figure," Crystal went on, "is that someone thought her shoes were my shoes. She put the tape on before the tryouts so she could cheat, and I wasn't ready for it."

"I didn't even consider that," Merry said.

It was the most logical explanation. Mallory stopped to consider why she hadn't thought of it herself. Just at that moment, Crystal gave a little shriek as Merry's eyes rolled up in her head. Before her twin could even take a step, Merry collapsed on the floor, hitting her head with a thunk that made even Mallory queasy.

Crystal would later tell Erika that Merry looked like a zombie chick or something from *Lost in the Hills.* She would tell Alli that she almost puked, although, in fact, she'd gone on eating her chocolates while a swarm of nurses squeezed into the room. Meredith woke looking up at a fat, red-faced nurse who stank of cigarettes. Her tummy rolled. Why did nurses smoke? Mallory was on the other side of the room, so pale she probably looked worse than Merry did, if possible.

How did Merry look? She'd done her hair carefully and picked out new five-pockets to go to Neely's. Now here she was, rolling in germs and about to have an egg on the back of her head that would really complement the scaly junk on her face.

"If you have anorexia, please don't come to our hospital and get hurt when you pass out from not eating!" the nurse said. "Look at your skin. That's from poor nutrition too."

Mallory said, "It is not! I'll have you know my sister eats more than most guys."

Thanks, sis, Merry thought, wishing she could add that Mallory, in fact, ate twice as much as most guys—and in front of them!

"Help me up," Merry said. "The red places on my face are from toothpaste. They have nothing to do with anything I ate," she told the nurse.

For a moment, Red-Faced Fat Person was clearly stumped. Then she started giving orders. "Don't move. You have to lie there until Dr. Pennington comes." Meredith knew Dr. Pennington. She'd fixed Adam's collarbone when he'd jumped out of the maple tree.

"It's not the first time," Mallory said helpfully. "Well, it is the first time for her. But I've fainted before." What was this? Mallory never spoke two sentences voluntarily to anyone but Meredith. But no sooner did the nurse look away than Mallory hissed at Merry, "Get up, imbecile! They'll think we really are on drugs! I'm trying to be nice to buy you time."

"What happened?"

"You fell over like somebody chopped you down, duh," Mallory whispered angrily.

"Well, you should know. It's your specialty."

"Not in front of fifty people," Mallory said.

"You mean, like not at my competition? Oh, there were only probably three hundred witnesses."

Mallory said, "Oh, my mistake. You only pass out in front of people who are trying to kill you!" Meredith took Mally's hand and stood up.

"That's AMG," the nurse said.

"What?"

"Against medical advice."

"Oh, stop," Merry said. "Will you go get my mother, please?"

"I'm sorry but I don't know your mother?" the nasty nurse said.

"She's Campbell Brynn? She's the chief nurse in the ER," Meredith said. Red-Face went white. Merry wanted to laugh. She personally would not have wanted to mess with Campbell's temper either.

"And I can't even see!" Crystal complained, trying to crane her neck around her suspended leg. "This is the first non-boring thing to happen since the anesthetic. Did you slip? How could you slip when I slipped? It's like a conspiracy or something."

That was exactly what it was, Merry thought. She had to get people to stop messing with her long enough to talk to her sister.

It *was* a conspiracy.

In her half-conscious vision, what she had seen were beautiful hands, tiny, each with two slim gold bands on the ring and index fingers. She saw those fingers lay two parallel slips of tape along the bottom of each tennis shoe and press the tape down securely. The giveaway was that when the hands set the shoes back up, Merry saw a tiny fish in permanent marker on the rubber tab. Fish was Crystal's last name. The mark was so small that anyone who didn't know wouldn't have noticed it. Crystal's hands were long and thin. The ones in Meredith's vision were elfin.

It had happened just like their theory. Someone had sabotaged Crystal. Her vision confirmed it. Meredith could only see the past. She'd seen hands that definitely were not Crystal's hands. She had to shuffle her mind like the bingo ball rollers they used at church when she went to bingo with Grandma Gwenny. She had to revise everything she had almost refused to believe but had nearly suspected about Neely. It had to be Neely, the overboard case of blond ambition. But how could it be Neely? She wasn't even on the squad. She wasn't allowed in the dressing room. She wouldn't have known where to look for the name tags that identified each girl's outfit, sewn in a tiny invisible flap in the hem of each garment.

Well, at least Merry would get the chance to find out tonight, literally first-hand. When she went to the sleepover, if Miss Richelle Rich said anything weird, or displayed a bunch of rings, Merry would just. . .have to find a way to stop her and make sure she got found out. There.

Someone wheeled a gurney into the room.

"No WAY!" Meredith said. "You heard my sister. I have a fainting disorder. We both do. I really am bulimic, anorexic, and neurotic! And psychotic! I need to have my father check me into a psychiatric hospital!"

"Really?" Crystal asked, almost climbing up the traction ropes to get a view. "You really are all those things? I know that Danielle's younger sister tried to be bulimic but it made her sick."

Crystal is such a genius, Merry thought; sometimes, Mallory was right about her friends.

"You're not going anywhere. You're Campbell's daughter, and you did this last spring," said a young guy who then identified himself as a medical student. "If we let you walk out of here, we might as well break our knees. She's down there in the ER waiting for you."

"No, no, no! I didn't do this last spring. That was my sister. We're twins," Merry pleaded. This day was morphing from fairly okay to epic-movie bad.

"We're having a brain panel done, Meredith Arness Brynn," Campbell said, appearing in the doorway. Apparently, she couldn't wait even for Merry to be wheeled down. "Mallory was too stubborn. At least it's convenient that you had *your* spell in the hospital. If this is something you and Mallory have going on, we'll get to the bottom of it!"

"Do you know that she's bulimic?" Crystal asked. Meredith tried to stare a hole into Crystal, but then observed that Crystal actually looked pretty loopy. The painkillers, no doubt.

"Thanks, Crystal, but we practically need a second mortgage to keep them both in chicken and pancakes."

"She probably just throws it all up," Crystal said.

"I'd know," Campbell said. "She'd have bad teeth."

"You can cover it up if you carry toothpaste," Crystal said.

"How do you know so much about it?" Mallory asked sweetly,

and Merry had never loved her twin more. Crystal made a face. Crystal had been a dancer since she was four. It was well-known that ballerinas were renowned pukers.

Merry said, "Mom, I'm not bulimic. And I didn't have a seizure." The gurney moved into the elevator and began to rocket drop to the basement, where the ER and operating rooms were.

"We know now that this probably isn't hormonal because you've already hit puberty," Campbell went on. "Although it could be . . ."

"Oh, kill me now," Merry said, her face the color of stewed beets. The intern, blond and athletic-looking, standing a foot away from her, was probably twenty. No, you couldn't be even a training doctor if you were only twenty. He was still young enough to give Merry a quiver in her stomach. After they got to the emergency room, Campbell hauled Merry behind a flimsy partition and held out one of those horrifying hospital gowns that showed your butt even if you weighed ninety pounds. Right in front of the cute-guy medical student.

"MOM! Let me go into the bathroom."

"You don't have anything no one's never seen," Campbell said. "It's just biology!"

This was their mother's favorite phrase. She ought to have the T-shirt.

"You're so sensitive, Mom!" Meredith snapped. "Like I want everyone to see mine again!"

A few hours later, Merry's perfectly, nicely made little pin-braids were matted and gluey from the eight million Frankenstein electrodes a technician stuck to her head before taking pictures of her brain. Mally had gone out into the lounge, at first whispering to her twin that she wished the pictures would show the part with the gift in it so they could both get it removed with a poke in the ear. Campbell e-mailed the results to a neurologist in Manhattan, and they all listened as he read them: no evidence of any history of seizures, no shadows that could be tumors. Unless the underlying cause was very, very subtle, there was no need for neurological follow-ups unless there was another event.

Mallory wandered into the room, rubbing her eyes.

"I was having my head examined and you were asleep?" Merry demanded. "What a leaker! Look at my hair! I have a sleepover to go to!"

"You're still going to go out . . . looking like . . . that? God, you are desperate," Mally said.

"Well, no, I would go home if I didn't have work to do! You know? If I'm going to . . . I have to tell you what I *think*, you know what I mean by *think*?" Merry asked. "I kind of have to go there if I *think* I could find out what happened at the tryouts. And I don't even have clothes, and Dad will probably bring me a pair of pajamas with duckies on them!"

"Oh, okay," Mallory apologized. "I didn't know you *thought* something. I really believed you fell over in there from natural causes. At least, I hoped it wasn't a . . . you know."

"She's got a pretty hard head. And I can't imagine what could be an emotional cause," Mally's mother said to Dr. Staats, the twins' pediatrician, who'd dropped by.

Dr. Staats asked, "No changes at home? No big upsets or events since that terrible business last year?"

Tim came in with a duffel for Merry. He gave Campbell the one look that parents don't know kids recognize for just what it is: something that they want kept secret. *There* is *something going on at home,* Merry thought. They were lying!

About what?

"No!" Merry said. "At least, I don't have any trouble." *That I can tell you about*, she thought. "It was Crystal's injury. It just made me woozy."

"Well . . ." Campbell said. "She's the sensitive one. When Mallory broke her leg, she thought that seeing bone protrude was interesting. Maybe it is emotional. I know how much emotional things can affect you physically."

Mom spoke so sweetly and sadly that both girls thought, *What's with her?* Did Campbell have an ulcer or something? Was Tim having an affair? Who'd have an affair with their father? When he wanted to get dressed up, he broke out a new ball cap.

Were they going to have something else to worry about?

Dark particles were whirling all around, and no one could see it except lucky people like Merry and Mallory. Couldn't it at least stay out of their house?

PAST OR FUTURE?

PAST OR FUTURE?

To their parents' shock, the twins willingly jumped into the way-back seat—the place they normally exiled Adam. They weren't out of the parking lot before Mallory whispered, "Okay, spill it. Now that I know you passed out because you saw, so what did you see?"

"Tape!" Merry said. "Tape on the bottom of somebody's shoe but not just that. I also saw her hands!"

"Did you see the lion flip over the shoes?" Mally asked.

"No. Just the tape on the shoes," Merry said. "But I saw someone doing it. Putting the tape on. Shut up about the lion. It's like mixing nuts and oranges."

"It's apples and . . . never mind. It's connected, Merry. I don't want to get started with this now, but I saw the lion once before in a dream. Eden knows about the lion somehow. And it made me think. Do you know what you saw, up on the ridge? What made David scream?"

"I don't. Just a flash of something. I try not to think about it. Did I even tell you I saw something?"

"Maybe you didn't tell me speeshaw. Ad nye blocken hearsen," Mally replied, slipping into twin tongue.

"Stop that," Campbell said automatically, with bionic hearing that screened out anything but what she wanted to hear. She turned the radio on.

"Okay. Maybe you heard me think about it. Whatever," Merry began again. "So you saw the cat twice, and you think it's connected or you think it's a coincidence?"

"I know it's connected. I just said I saw it before, flathead! I saw it then, past tense, and now, present tense. Now, as in a couple of weeks ago. Then, as in up on a ridge, last winter. And I think it really was up on the ridge when David died. And . . . Eden has something to do with it."

"Pull in here," Campbell called out suddenly, as they passed Dean's Dairy Den. "Tim, I want a green-tea milk-shake and fries with barbecue sauce. I heard that Shelby Dean will add any flavor you want now. Maybe I'll have green tea and chocolate."

"Oh gag!" Adam cried. "I'll have a normal milk-shake and stand outside the car."

"Mom," Merry whined professionally. "I'm already years late for this sleepover! Can't you go after you drop me off?"

Campbell sighed, then nodded. Tim drove on toward Haven Hills.

Merry dropped her voice again. She asked her twin, "Eden? Why Eden? She's not a cheerleader."

"I don't know. But it was a cheerleader's shoe that the lion flipped over."

"Did it see tape on the shoe?" Merry asked. "You didn't see the mountain lion look at tape on a shoe?"

"Who could see tape on a shoe? It's invisible!" Mallory wanted to jump out of the car. They were already in the housing development and had so little time left to talk.

"Anyhow, I didn't see the lion when I fell in Crystal's hospital room," Meredith said. "I only saw someone's hands putting the tape on. And I think I know whose. I think I'm staying over tonight at her house."

"For real? You think it was Neely? You said no way before."

"Well, I don't know how she would have known who to try to hurt. I haven't figured that out. But whoever I saw had little hands, like mine and yours. Who else has little hands? Alli? Kim? I know it wasn't them. The hands had gold rings. Really pretty gold rings. Crystal never wears rings. And who else could afford them? Even if they're cheapie gold, they'd be ten bucks each. Who has eighty dollars to spend on little rings?"

"So we're going to find out if Neely did it, and if she's going to do it again. And if she is . . ."

"I'll stop her."

"Merry, wow," Mallory said admiringly. "That's having some sand." She was quiet for a moment. "I hate to have to tell you this but, you know I fell asleep out there," Mallory admitted. "I was just tired. I didn't think I'd dream. But I did, and I saw hands putting tape on a shoe too."

"You mean we had the same dream?"

"Not the same dream," Mallory said. "It means that it happened once. . . ."

"And it's going to happen again in the future, obviously," Merry went on. She drew a deep breath. "Well. So I know what's what. I know what I have to do."

They both fell silent.

"Do you think you might be in some danger, Ster?" Mallory asked. "You know, you're her rival too. There are swimming pools there in her house and stuff."

"Come on, she's not trying to kill me, Mal. Don't be dramatic. I'll be fine. Alli and Caitlin will be there. I wouldn't go alone."

"It's bugging me. Rings? Who wears rings? Who's changed styles?" Mallory said. "I don't pay attention to that stuff. I wouldn't notice if Alli had her hair dyed green. I can't think of anyone who wears rings." She punched her hand. "I can't think at all."

"Well, it doesn't have to be a cheerleader. It could be somebody else completely. Like someone who's just pissed because a girl broke up with him. It could be a whole other agenda."

"But who else would care enough to do something like that? Look at Crystal. I know she's kind of dumb and conceited but . . . the poor girl. No one deserves that. And I should know what the connection is with Eden and the lion by now, but I don't have a clue. How does it all fit?"

Her sister said, with a sigh, "I so do not want to find out. But that would hint that I had a choice about finding out. Which I don't."

"Look both ways tonight."

"I will," Merry said. She was used to Mallory being the tough one. Block by block, she lost her nerve. And on top of that, she grew more self-conscious. Goo in her hair. Wrinkled, sweaty clothes. She hoped they'd go swimming right away so no one would notice.

At least, she thought, *this whole little matter will be over tonight.*

A sad and painful thing for Crystal, but a piece of cake compared with last year.

Long afterward, Merry would look back and realize that she had allowed hope to triumph over instinct. She was so eager to see a simple ending—or any ending—that she had mistaken a cliff for a cul-de-sac.

THE NEELY FACTOR

N ow, that's some shack," said Tim.

It was the first time that either Mally or Meredith had gotten more than a passing glance at the Chaplins' new home. They'd seen it under construction several times, on the way to their grandparents' house, but everyone at school had heard about the sauna, Neely's second-floor workout room, and how the indoor pool had a lane that opened to the outdoor pool.

Grandpa Arthur Brynn, their father's father, and his mom, Grandma Gwenny-—the one who was from a long line of psychics— lived in Bell Fields, next to Haven Hills. And he had no use for these huge houses; he called them power guzzlers. Grandpa used to complain that all the young families were leaving Ridgeline, but now the town council Grandpa chaired was considering zoning rules to keep the population under control and stop more farms from becoming developed. People like the Chaplins, who moved from Chicago when her father's business relocated to New York City, thought Ridgeline was "cute," Grandpa Arty said, like some fairy-tale country town. When Dad's brother Uncle Kevin pointed out that their money was as green as anyone else's—probably more so—Grandpa stomped out to the back of the yard to smoke a cigar.

Still, who needed a seven-thousand-square-foot house? Some of the old folks said the Chaplin house was a *two-acre* house on a *three-acre* lot, although people knew they were exaggerating.

Neely had one stepbrother, Casey, a graduate student who didn't come to visit much. There were eight bedrooms. Neely's "suite" was the highlight—from the computer and music-mixing station to the bathroom bigger than most bedrooms to the weight equipment that had to have been lifted up the stairs by a crane or something. "She has a weight machine and a treadmill and an elliptical and a Pilates Cadillac," Erika raved. "She doesn't even have to walk upstairs to take a shower."

"Wonder how much all this set them back," Campbell said, perusing the expanse of champagne brick and fieldstone.

Tim replied cheerfully, "More than we'll ever see. What do you think they do?"

"Sell drugs," said Campbell.

"Mom!" Mallory and Merry gasped together.

"I didn't mean it," Campbell told them. "It was a figure of speech."

Meredith jumped out of the car and began running up the drive, which she quickly noticed had the pitch of a ski hill. She yelled back, "I'll be polite! Call me if you need me! I have my phone. I'm not sick, so don't worry. The meds they gave me are working now and I can hardly feel it."

"You don't have your pajamas, though," Tim called after her. Merry stopped. "I brought your flannel pants and your Giants sweatshirt."

"Did you bring my iPod, Dad?" Meredith asked.

"You go to somebody's house for a sleepover and listen to music they can't hear? Isn't that rude?"

"Why?" Meredith asked.

Just then, Neely pulled up in a four-seater golf cart, with Alli and Caitlin in the back.

"I saw you down here struggling," she said. "Hi, Merry's parents! I'm Cornelia Chaplin." Neely shook hands as though she were twenty-five. She turned to Merry. "We thought we'd come and get you. If I had to walk up that driveway every day, I'd expire."

"You work harder in practice than you do walking up the drive," Campbell said mildly.

"But that's just what I mean! If Merry leads practice, I'm wrung out like a rag when I get home," Neely said.

What a suck-up, Mallory thought.

But Merry thought Neely was being really nice, in a phony way.

"Well, have a nice time!" Campbell said. "I should have spoken to your parents."

"Oh, they're here! And we will!" Neely called.

"Merry, you take it easy," Campbell said. "You know you have a concussion at least. You should be at home. This is ridiculous."

"My dad is setting up a movie, and we have cheese and shrimp puffs from Luda. It's going to be a laid-back night," answered Neely. "Don't worry."

"Well," said Campbell, "I'm only ten minutes away. Call before you go to sleep or if you have any changes in vision or increased pain."

"Does she always talk like that?" Neely asked, as they spun away.

Alli and Caitlin said together, "Yes."

Luda must be some fancy restaurant in New York City, Meredith thought.

As they sped up the drive, with Meredith clinging to her duffel with one hand, Caitlin chattered, "We already went swimming. You should see the pool. It's as big as the one at school! There's a twelve-foot end and a diving board."

"We can go again later," Neely said. "But I have to eat now. Swimming makes me starved. We thought you would be here sooner."

"I was, uh, I was in the hospital. Witness my hair."

"I thought Crystal was in the hospital," Neely said.

"Well, we went to see Crystal and her leg was gross and I guess I just passed out," Merry explained.

"It was that gross?" Alli asked. "Warn me, because I'm going to see her tomorrow after practice."

"It wasn't gross to see. It was the way she described the ligaments being torn."

"I thought passing out was Mallory's thing," Caitlin said. To Neely, she said, "Remember? Mallory's her twin. She faints all the time."

"Does she have, like, a brain problem?" Neely asked.

"No," Merry answered.

"Yes," said Alli.

A guy in a coat and jeans had come to take the golf cart away. Neely said, "Thanks, Stuart."

A servant!

Campbell refused even to hire a house cleaner, pointing out that the girls had arms and could push a vacuum. Merry told Neely, "They just like to get down on Mallory because she plays soccer, and she thinks cheerleaders are ga-ga. And no, she doesn't have epilepsy or anything, and neither do I. I just got woozy because of Crystal's leg, and then I had to hang around for ages to get a brain test and junk. My mom's so overprotective she's paranoid."

"They had to test your brain?" Neely asked.

"Well, it could have been a seizure. But it wasn't." Merry pointed to her head. "Hence the nice hair gel."

"It's a very fresh look," Alli said and broke the tension. "I'm glad you're okay, Mer. But you can see the lump on your head from here. It's going to kill in the morning."

"I have ice packs and they gave me some super strong acetaminophen and codeine."

"What?" Neely asked.

"Her mom's a nurse," Caitlin said. "She can't say 'aspirin' like a regular person."

The girls ran up a staircase that looked like it was out of one of the old movies Campbell forced them to see, like *Gone with the Wind*. Neely's room was like an apartment, with her own projection TV and two computers, one just for mixing music. The viewing system was elaborate, with speakers in alcoves all over the room. This was what Neely meant by her dad "setting up" a movie. There was an actual little projector-type thing, not a DVD player. The whole other side was the fabled closet with buttons Neely could push to make the racks move so that she could choose clothes by color.

Then came Neely's actual bedroom. It wasn't really a "room," the way the other girls understood it. It was a "suite" of small rooms —almost like her own little apartment in the gigantic house.

Everything that draped or floated around the king-sized bed was peach and black. Peach sheets with a black velvet comforter. Peach curtains encircling the bed that swept down from a star-shaped light on the ceiling. Black velvet pillows and bolsters. In one corner, Meredith glimpsed an open door that led to a bathtub so big it needed steps to get into it.

"This is a lot like our room," Merry said. She thought of their corner of the attic with one dresser in one closet and the private bathroom they were so proud of in the other closet and wanted to fall on the floor laughing.

"It is?"

"Oh, please. My room is in the attic. It's not a hole in the wall. It's a hole in the roof!"

"You live in a big house," Alli said loyally.

"It's big, but it's old-big. . . . There are a bunch of goofy little rooms they used to keep canned berries and bags of potatoes in and stuff a hundred years ago. Literally a hundred years ago. And something is always breaking. This house . . . this is like the mall," Merry said. "I share a room with my sister."

"I couldn't stand sharing a room," Neely said. "I have to have absolute darkness and quiet when I sleep because I'm so wound up. I have to wear a sleep mask."

Merry said, "But it's so quiet here at night. It's hard to believe, living here, that people take the train to New York every day."

Neely said, "They wanted me to have country air. I loved city air."

"We like being close to New York but not in it," Caitlin said.

"Well, you see, Chicago, in a lot of ways, was more cutting-edge than New York. Like fashion, for example."

"Like that's nuts, for example," said Alli, defending her city. "If Chicago is so about clothes, why does, like, Ralph Lauren live in New York? Is he still alive?"

Nobody was sure, but they knew he had lived in New York, or at least New Jersey.

"You've never been to Chicago," Neely said softly. She didn't elaborate. Was it really just an explanation or a whole new form of snottiness? If it was, Merry wanted to learn it: All three of the girls from Ridgeline had just got spanked somehow, and they didn't even feel it.

Mrs. Chaplin ("Call me CeeCee . . . . "), who had her own online hat and jewelry boutique, and whose black velvet leggings with a green velvet riding jacket and a huge suede hat were the talk of the town, stopped in. She was as thin as one of the girls. "I'm going to do my yoga practice, Neely, love. Do you girls want some pizza puffs to go with the shrimp?" she asked.

"We're fine, Mama. We're going to watch the movie." Mrs. Chaplin wiggled her fingers in farewell. Neely dimmed the lights. "This is such a cool little indie. It's not in theaters yet. It's about this girl who runs away from a religious commune with her boyfriend."

"How did you get it?" Alli asked.

"My dad's one of the producers," Neely said. "He does a lot of little things besides entertainment law. He produces movies. He's working on a book about renewable energy. He's the lawyer for mostly directors and stuff but some movie stars too. Like, I used to think Demi Moore was my aunt or something."

Merry said, "Oh."

"Where did you get these?" Alli asked of the shrimp puffs. "These are so great I could, like, live on them. Is Luda a caterer?"

"No! Luda's a person. Ludamila. She's from Georgia, not the state—the country by Russia. Luda's lived with us since I was born."

"And Stuart?"

"He's her husband. Sergei. He changed it when they became citizens. He works here too. And then I have tutors and my gym coach. She comes once a week from the city. And the cleaners and my mom's assistant, Natalie."

"You have your own coach? Like . . . no class?" Caitlin asked.

Neely smiled. "My mother was an Embraceable You when she was young. Before she met my father."

"A what?" Meredith asked.

"A St. Louis Rams cheerleader. A professional cheerleader," Neely answered. "She was teaching me style things when I was in preschool."

"They're called the You's, like the You's and Me's?" Caitlin asked.

"No. E-W-E. It's a female ram."

Imagine living this way, Merry thought. It was like Neely was princess of something. She imagined even being an only child, without the constant emotional noise of Mallory's moods and Adam's pranks. What she felt stunned her: For a moment that fluttered past like the flap of a wing, she missed Mallory.

"Forget the movie! Let's do something!" Neely said. "I require action."

Neely opened her makeup cabinet, where Merry could see boxed sets in gold or turquoise packages, unopened. Neely took out a length of silver tasseled braid, which she attached to a roofing nail under the windowsill. She filled a backpack with rolls of toilet paper and helped the others, one by one, slide down to the ground, showing them how to leap the beams of the motion detectors so no lights went on when they slid the golf cart out onto Woods Meadow Road.

"Andy Wegner is that cute junior, right?" Neely asked. "His father is the club pro? They live right behind us."

For the next fifteen minutes, Neely and the others festooned the

Wegners' house and trees with roll after roll of toilet paper that waved in the mild night breeze like the sails of tiny ships.

"He'd kill you if he knew it was you!" Caitlin said.

"Oh no! He'd be flattered," Neely said. "Who else can we do?"

Forty minutes and three more cute guys' houses later, the girls rope-climbed back into Neely's room, where cups of hot chocolate were magically waiting. Neely replaced the silver braid and took out a small bottle of Bailey's Irish Cream. Of all of them, Alli usually pretended to be the most sophisticated, but even her eyes popped. She asked, "Don't they see that stuff? I mean Luda cleans in here, right?"

"My parents can handle it," Neely said. "We're totally honest with each other. They know a person has to cut loose once in a while. If you get to do a little now, you won't be tempted to do a lot later. I stay in limits."

"My life would be limited," said Merry. "To about five minutes."

"So tell me stuff," said Neely as they sipped. "Tell me all the bad things that happened before I came. I know Kim's older brother died. Was it in the Middle East?"

Her eyes seemed to glitter. Was gossip like this what she thought of as fun? About somebody's dead brother? Merry wondered what Neely would think of as a really bad thing to do. . . . Merry thought of the little fingers, with their rings.

"He fell off a cliff, up above the river," Caitlin began slowly, before Merry could shush her. "Meredith was there. Tell her, Mer."

"There's not that much to tell. I heard him scream. It wasn't suicide. No one thinks that. It was a total accident. I just called the police."

"And now Kim's doing weird stuff," Caitlin said suddenly. "She's hanging with boys from Deptford and going to the quarry."

Going to the quarry was code. It was code for using drugs. None of them knew what kind of drugs they were, but everyone knew they were the dangerous kind, and the girls who went there would be pregnant by sophomore year.

"Kim wouldn't do that," Merry objected. The shrimp and cheese were too rich for her stomach, and the house suddenly seemed too hot.

"You don't know her anymore," Caitlin said.

Merry thought, *Do I?*

She didn't feel as though she knew very much about anything.

For one thing, she'd never had more than a sip of champagne. Downing at least three little cups of Bailey's in her mug tasted great with the hot choc, but she was woozy. She got up and splashed her face.

It did no good.

"I'm so exhausted," she told the others, who were now preparing facial goop in a marble basin. "It must be from the hospital. I have to rest for a little while."

Nearly stumbling, Merry fell into her own queen-sized pouf of a bed, which had been prepared for her while they were out TP-ing.

She heard the others laughing and trying to decide between mint-jasmine and honey-butter-cream scrub.

Merry was asleep when she walked over to the window and looked down—although she didn't know it. She thought she was sleepwalking, although she later found out that her feet had never touched the floor. Merry looked down and saw that she wore a white gown with blue satin behind the eyelet lace—the kind of gown that probably cost fifty dollars. Out across the expanse of dark lawn were the ranks of the Chaplins' trees, the moon between them like a ball tossed nervously hand to hand. But beyond the trees, it was morning.

There was Mallory, running—her hair pulled back in a nubby ponytail, her sweatshirt tied around her waist. The leaves were green. It was summer beyond the Chaplins' lawn. Up into the hills Mally magically ascended, and as Merry watched, her hands pressed against the glass—so cool to her palms it seemed real—the scrub trees next to the path parted, and the huge white lion, four times Mallory's size, stepped out into the path behind her sister. It took a few slow steps, then broke into a lope, slowly gaining on Mallory—who seemed unaware that anything was there.

"Mallory! Siow!" Merry shouted.

She began to hammer the glass, harder and harder.

Mallory didn't hear her. The lion loped closer, then closer . . . .

"Merry! Wake up! Merry!" Neely was holding Merry's arms down at her sides. "You're having a nightmare."

"I was? My arms . . . are so tired. I don't feel like I was even really asleep."

"You were rolling and thrashing around."

"I'm sorry," Merry said. "Did I wake anyone else up?"

"No, they're out cold, and I wasn't even asleep yet," Neely said. "Do you want some water or some hot chocolate?" Neely's hazel eyes, so haughty in daylight, were soft and gentle with concern. "You were crying too, Merry."

"I'm okay," said Merry. "It was the Bailey's. I felt so strange, I must have dreamed I got up."

But when Merry looked down, her breath stopped for an instant and then began to come faster and faster. For when she put her hands together, she saw that her fingers were bruised, as if she really had pounded madly on panes of glass.

EDEN'S GIFT

The following Sunday was the big fall sidewalk sale, the biggest day of the year at Domino Sports. Mally was out in front, stacking shoe boxes in a pyramid, when she heard a soft voice behind her murmur her name.

Eden.

"Hi," she said. "Boo. Aren't you going to run away?"

Mallory shocked herself by starting to cry, making this about five times more than she'd cried in the previous five years.

"Eden, I didn't mean to."

Quiet for a moment, Eden nodded. "I know that. I know why you did."

"But there's no reason for me to be afraid of you."

"Well, there is, Mallory. I have to be afraid of the same things about me that you do. But I would never hurt you or your sister or anyone you love. No matter what it cost me. And it could cost me everything." She held up one hand. "I can't tell you any more. It's just like you can't tell people about you and Merry. Do you trust me?" Eden's eyes grew darker and brighter, like wet stones.

"Of course I do," Mallory said.

"Help me find a sleeping bag."

"I already have one picked out," Mally told her. "It's wrapped and in the back."

"It's a Christmas present, but I'm so excited I might have to give it to him before. How much is it?" Eden asked. It was filled with two kinds of down and cost $299 on sale. Mallory counted up what was in her own bank account. She was a bit of a hoarder, and Eden couldn't read minds. "It's a hundred dollars!"

"Oh, Mallory! That's less than I thought! How long is it going to take you to stack those shoes?"

"Years. I haven't even got the ladder yet," Mally said.

"Well, it helps to have tall friends," Eden said, laughing as she attacked the four-sided pyramid. "I'm putting the fives on top. Who wears size five? Cinderella?"

"Me," Mallory admitted.

As they worked, Eden explained, "You know that the cat is a symbol, right? We're Bear Clan, my family, but the mountain lion is a symbol of power. In the old times, people thought human beings would shift into animals, and that shape-shifters—that's what they were called—brought luck to the tribe. It's like mythology. Every tribe has stories like that one. They're like the stories in the Bible."

"How," Mally asked, "did you have any idea I was thinking about the mountain lion?"

Eden sighed. "A guess. You brought up the dream when I talked about James. You know, all people have their superstitions. Your family has superstitions, right?"

"You could call them that," Mallory said, standing on tiptoe to hand Eden another box.

"Eden," Tim said. "I was coming out here to help this one finish up the stack but I guess she doesn't need me."

"Hi, Mr. Brynn."

"We've got your pretty red sleeping bag all wrapped up in back. Must be one special couple for you to spend—"

"Dad!" Mallory warned Tim.

"Oh, right," Mally's father said, without quite knowing why he was agreeing. "Uh-oh. Here come the Delsandros. All five boys. Five bats, five cleats, five jerseys."

"I'll be right in, Dad," said Mallory.

"No, it's good. The store is pretty quiet otherwise. Mrs. Delsandro's got a system with those kids. She must assign them numbers, like you get at a deli. Besides them, there's just Caitlin and Jackie browsing for two hours."

When the jingle of the door and Tim's hearty call engulfed Mrs. Delsandro and the five boys, Eden said, "Then you get that it's not real."

"The mountain lion? Sure. But I ran because I dreamed about the cougar again just the other night! I dreamed it was in school!" Eden took a deep breath and looked away. "I was scared. There was an accident after I had that dream. And I thought the lion was bad luck."

"It is bad luck. Some things that are very powerful are also bad luck. But . . . not for you."

"How do you know?"

"I . . . it's my superstition. I just know. Can you go just around the corner and get a coffee?" Eden asked. Mallory held up her hands to her father, signifying she'd be back in ten minutes. In the Latte Beans drive-through, Eden ordered two large green-tea lattes, with extra whip. Handing Mally one, she said, "My treat."

Mallory took a long drink to make sure her voice wouldn't sound like a rusty door opening.

"Do they want you away from James because he's not, you know . . . ?"

"Not an Indian? No! But he's not afraid of them . . . like most people." Eden laughed but it wasn't pretty. "Most people think that if my family gets mad they'll kill them with tomahawks or something. Even you probably, and you're one of my closest friends."

"Eden! I'm not like that!" Mallory was reeling from hearing Eden say that she, little Mally, was one of Eden's closest friends.

"You'd be surprised what people think if you're not just like them," Eden said, as Mallory thought, *No, I wouldn't*. "But yes, the present is a secret. My family doesn't want me to date anyone! They wouldn't care if he was Geronimo."

"Geronimo?" Mallory asked. It was the first time she'd heard the name other than hearing someone in one of Adam's idiot shows yell it when he was jumping out of a tree.

"The great Apache warrior. Goyaase. Don't you know any American history but George Washington?" Eden winced. "I'm sorry, Mally. My whole . . . life is getting on my nerves."

"Tell me about it," Mally said. "Mine too."

"Strict is one thing but . . . they'll go hysterical if I fall in love, ever. It's not just James."

"You mean in high school."

"You'll never get it," Eden said with a sigh.

"You're exaggerating."

"Are you exaggerating?" Eden asked. "Like, how you look right now. You didn't sleep. You're so tweaked about something you saw."

Mally curled a strand of her hair around one finger before she said, "Eden, you're the best friend I have, except Drew. Or you were. I can't stand that you don't like me anymore."

"What? Of course I like you, Mal," Eden said. "I just understand why you'd want to avoid me."

"Avoid you? Edes, you wouldn't let me apologize." Eden put her hands over her ears. "Friends don't lie to each other. I couldn't tell you that I *didn't* feel danger from the cat."

"Don't, Mallory. Don't."

"Okay, I won't!" Mallory said. Why did any mention of this myth upset her so, if it was only a myth?

"I love James, Mallory. I only get to see him part of the year because he works in New Mexico in spring and summer. But I truly love him."

"How could you know that when you were only fourteen when you met him?"

Eden smiled slowly and, after a moment of hesitation, reached over and lightly hugged Mallory's shoulders. She said, "You just know." Mally made a hoovering noise with her straw. Both girls laughed. "Or maybe not!"

"So you forgive me?"

"There's nothing to forgive."

Back at the store, Eden and Mally carefully opened a corner of the package so Eden could see the lush heft and color of the sleeping bag. She smiled like she'd been accepted to Harvard.

"Thank you so much, Mal. And don't worry about the other thing anymore, okay? It scares everyone."

"You mean, other people have the same dream?" Mallory asked.

"No," Eden said. "I didn't mean that."

"What did you mean?"

"Mallory, can't you just please stop asking?"

"That's like telling me to stop caring!"

"Then stop caring!"

"I can't do that," Mallory said.

"You'll be sorry," Eden said.

Mallory said, "I know that."

POWWOW

After practice the following Saturday, Eden pulled Mallory aside.

"Do you want to go to a powwow?" she asked.

"I'd go to a luau," Mallory told her. "I'm sorry, but I need some distraction. Not only did I spend two straight days of twelve hours selling tennis shoes to bratty kids, I had two term papers due and . . ." *And then there was worrying as a second job,* she thought, but didn't say.

"Well, it's the harvest powwow, and it's Friday night. I have to do things for it so I can't pick you up, but if your dad can drive you, I'll bring you back the next morning." *The next morning? Eden is asking me to sleep over?* "Nobody does much sleeping. But bring your sleeping bag!" Eden grinned as she grabbed her towel and shampoo. "You can't use mine. It's special!"

"What . . . what should I wear? Do I have to dress up?"

Eden answered, but her words were lost in the rush and shout of the shower. Mallory waited patiently. It was a rank thing that the older girls got to shower first, and the younger ones usually put up with cold water or waited until they got home. Later Eden came outside in a camisole and sweats.

"I didn't hear you. About what I should wear," Mally murmured.

"Well, you wear ceremonial clothes, of course. You have ceremonial clothes, right?" Eden asked. Mallory smiled weakly. Eden laughed. "Jeans and a nice shirt, Mally! You goof! And a long coat! Plan on it getting dirty! You'll be sitting on the ground outside if it's nice, around a fire."

"Good deal," Mallory said.

Tim pulled up then. Mallory made a motion for him to roll down the window and leaned in. "I'm going to . . . I mean, can I go to the powwow at Eden's house on Friday?" Mally asked.

"I . . . well, I'll ask Mom, but sure," Tim said.

"And don't forget a pillow!" Eden said. "There's never enough to go around."

"Why do you need a pillow?" Meredith asked.

"I'm staying over there. I always bring my own pillow."

"What always? You've never stayed—"

"Shut up, Meredith."

"Don't talk to your sister that way," Tim warned her. "Apologize."

"Sorry, Merry. Sorry that you have a big mouth."

"My brother Cooper will be home. I haven't seen him for a year! I'm pumped!" Eden said.

"Where is he?" Mally asked.

"He's at Boston Flanders."

"What's that?"

"It's a prep school," Tim said admiringly. "Don't worry. You guys will never go. It's, like, thirty big ones a year."

"Not if you're American Indian. They think so few of us are smart that he gets in free!" Eden said. "You become fluent in a language. You get to travel six weeks every year. Like, to Japan or to Italy."

"Cool," Merry said.

"He got a scholarship. He started last year," Eden said proudly.

"Does he like it?" Tim asked.

"It was really hard for him at first. When you're from a big family, it's hard to separate." Eden began to climb into the truck she called Godzilla, which had replaced her battered blue pickup.

"Okay! Well, I'll be there!"

As they pulled away, Tim's phone *brrrr*ed with his tone, "Purple Haze."

Campbell wanted pizza with no cheese and extra onions.

"Blech," Merry said. "Can we get some normal pizza too? What's wrong with Mom? Is she on an ulcer diet?"

"Extra onions?" Tim asked. "That wouldn't be indicative of an ulcer. No, she's got a little bug. But it's temporary. Don't worry." Into the cell phone, he said, "Yes, Campbell. I will hurry. The girls are already in the car. We were talking to Eden Cardinal about a powwow. Yes, of course her parents will be there. It's a family thing, Campbell. Even I know that much." Tim slipped the phone into his pocket. "How old is Eden's brother?"

"Sixteen," said Merry from the backseat.

"How do you know?"

"I texted Alli. She remembers him from her class in middle school. He's really cute. Or he was then. Maybe he's fat now."

"Why do you say such things? Can't you even keep your cell phone mouth shut? This is about *my* friend, Meredith."

"Soooorreeeeee," Meredith said with perfect insincerity. "It's not like you have that many."

"No," Mallory said. "Just the best ones."

PRINCESS

The night of the powwow was warm and golden—Indian summer for sure, Mally thought, as her father drove her out past the Catholic Church and down the pitted road that led to Eden's family farm. Tim couldn't get too close, because there were cars parked across the road for what seemed like a mile—rows of vans and junky souped-up old Buicks teenage boys would have, and here and there a new Lexus that Tim would have liked to test-drive—all lined up every which way.

"I can walk from here, Dad," Mallory said. "The houses are right up there. It's probably a couple of blocks."

"If there wasn't a moon, you couldn't see your hand in front of your face out here," Tim said. "It's eerie. Do you have your cell phone?"

"Dad," Mallory chided him. "Do you think Eden would let anything bad happen to me?"

"People drink a lot at these things."

"People drink a lot at your Christmas party."

"Truer words," Tim agreed, thinking of his own air-guitar rendition of "Free Bird" at the last Domino Sports holiday bash. "I'm sorry. Just be careful."

"Dad! Merry sleeps over at six different people's houses a month! Do you ever give her the third degree? Eden doesn't live on Pilgrim Street or Cedar or Oak. It's because she's different from Merry's friends."

"Okay! Okay!" Tim held his hands up in surrender.

"Eden will bring me home in the morning. Actually, we'll probably drop by just long enough for me to get my gear because we have practice at ten."

"Have fun."

"I'm excited."

"I wonder what they do at a powwow."

"Dance, I guess. I know they eat a lot. Eden told me there's a drum circle."

"I'd like to see that," Tim admitted.

"I'll take a picture with my cell phone."

"Don't want your dad along, huh? Even for a minute?"

"Nothing personal," said Mally. Tim kissed her.

Mallory tried to hurry. But though her spirit wanted to go join the festival, her body balked. Every step felt heavier, going toward the place where Eden was loved, where Eden was happy.

Why?

The fat russet moon made the red-dirt road as clear to see as though it were late afternoon. Mally hurried toward the lights. A group of men stood laughing and smoking cigars at the edge of the property. Some wore jeans and T-shirts and sport coats, others long flannel shirts. Some had braided hair longer than Eden's.

"Hello," one said. "Are you looking for Ayana?" Ayana was Eden's cousin, a seventh grader.

"No, I'm Eden's friend, Mallory Brynn."

"Mallory!" said a tall man, stepping forward from the group. "I'm Emmett Cardinal, Eden's dad. She's told me a lot about you. Welcome to our home." He put out his huge hand and Mallory took it. Just then, another group of family members arrived, the father carrying a long leather coat in his arms.

"Emmett! What a perfect night! Where is Ahtakahoop? We brought this for him all the way from New York!"

"A full-length leather coat!" said Mallory.

"Don't be too impressed. That's my nephew's business, making leather clothes. It's for Ahtakahoop, my son who's home from school in Boston. His birthday is Halloween."

"Ahtak . . . ?" Mally began.

"Cooper," said Eden's father, beginning to lead her toward the back of the property. "That's what most people outside the family call him. Coop. Ahtakahoop means 'star blanket.'"

"Eden said that. She meant the sky."

"Well, yes," said Eden's father. "This is the hunter's moon. What does 'Mallory' mean?"

"Some people say it means 'valiant, brave'. But it also means 'unlucky'," Mallory admitted. "It's a Welsh name."

"Well, you use it for the first meaning," Mr. Cardinal said. "Edensau is right up there, in the long house, helping her mother and aunts lay out the feast. They're late with it as usual. They work a little and then they talk. I'm lucky! My job was over when my brothers and I built the longhouse!"

The longhouse was set in a stand of birch trees and looked almost like a giant tent. From what Mallory could see, it was made of bent tree limbs in a frame that probably was twenty feet high to form a curved roof, like the bottom of a boat. Birch bark framed the windows and the roof; but the rest of the house was made of some kind of waterproof canvas, like a raincoat big enough to cover a blue whale. Smoke issued from a hole in the exact center of the roof, where a modern tin chimney was built in. Jack-o'-lanterns carved with suns, moons, bears, and birds lined up against the front wall beneath the windows. The effect was of forty delicate party lanterns in the dark.

Mallory stepped inside.

"*Tanisi*, Mallory!" a voice called.

Eden was pretty; everyone said so. But she usually dressed as plainly as Mally. If she wore makeup, it was a touch of lip gloss. Tonight, Eden's lashes were thick and black and straight as tiny fans. She had colored her lips with a berry tint. A subtle sweep of blue shadow made her brown eyes bigger and brighter, and her black lashes stood out like thick wings.

What a knockout woman Eden would be. What a knockout woman Eden already was.

She wore a long white sleeveless dress beaded by hand with blue whorls and spirals, which Mally could see represented the outlines of hills and trees and . . . long-legged creatures. Her laced white boots were fitted close to her slim but muscled soccer-jock legs, and a blue shawl was pinned with a gold star. In her hair were tiny plaits, little braids made by fairy fingers, beaded in gold, white, blue, and black.

Mallory cried out, "Edes, you look like . . . like a goddess or something."

Eden's smile was so sad. Why?

"*Tanisi* is Cree for hello, Mal! Come and meet my family."

Mallory had soon lost track of the number of names and hugs— from at least fifty women and girls to a dozen toddlers, too little to run outside with the bigger ones. Some of the children had ordinary names, like Brian and Hailey. Others were called Samash and Shilah.

"Did someone scare you so much, you stopped growing?" Eden's aunt Patricia asked.

"Auntie!" Eden reproved a big-shouldered woman with a sweep of silvery hair. Like many of the other women, she wore a floor-length cotton dress that reminded Mallory vaguely of Hawaiian clothing she'd seen in pictures.

Eden's mother, Wenona, wore a blue dress with long sleeves, patterned with white moons. "She's teasing, Mally!"

"This is all the taller I get!" Mallory answered, shrugging. "I'm a twin. We come in size small!"

"And every inch of that is muscle," Eden said. "Mallory is our star midfielder." All the women and girls murmured and smiled.

"Well, feed her and she'll grow!" Eden's mom said. The table was spread with every kind of food Mallory had ever seen and some she hadn't—berry pies and fried snowflake doughnuts, turkey slices and venison steaks, bread baked in the shapes of foxes, wolves, and bears.

"Our surprise first, Mama," Eden said. "Come with me."

Eden led Mallory up the back stairs of her family's house. Unfolding a sheaf of tissue, she held up a heavy cotton dress, black with silver birds embroidered on each shoulder. She lifted out a pair of black leather moccasins beaded with the same pattern. "I know that Brynn means 'bird' or 'dark wing'. But my grandmother likes silver best. She made these for you to wear tonight."

"But I can't. I might spill," Mallory said. "She *made* shoes?" People *made* jam. Aunt Kate and Grandma Gwenny made sweaters and hats and mittens. But shoes? That was like saying Eden's grandmother had whipped up a little car for Mallory to drive around during the party.

"They're *for* you. They're yours to keep. We made them for you. I helped her bore the holes for the stitching. She won't use a leather punch from the craft store at the mall. She has to do it the old-fashioned way, each hole punched with a sharpened hook made of shell."

"I can't accept these, Eden! These would cost . . . a hundred dollars!"

"More than that. Grandmere sells them to museums. There are three hundred acres out here and thirty kids in the six houses. How do you think they feed them all? It's not just by selling Christmas trees!"

"And that's more reason! I just can't!"

"Mally. White people bring things to people's houses for a party. We give away. We give a gift to everyone who comes. Yours is special. Try it on."

Mallory let the dress rustle softly over her head.

"Now close your eyes," said Eden, taking Mally's hand and leading her. When Mallory opened her eyes, in front of an ancient mirror, she gasped. She looked like something she had never considered herself to be.

Pretty.

"Oh, Mally. Grandmere was right."

"Is this what Indian princesses wear?"

"There's no such thing as an Indian princess!" Eden laughed. "Indians are what's called matriarchal. At least our tribe is. That means the men bring the fish, but the magic is in the women. When the men drum, they sing about women, strong women with straight backs who bring magic. Magic not like tricks but like good luck. Medicine is . . . good magic. Happiness and fortune. You don't have to get all the old symbolism. You just have to feel pretty."

"How did you make the shoes fit me?" Mally asked.

"Remember? Nobody wears size five except Cinderella."

"You're a trickster!" Mally said.

"Why did you say that?" Eden asked sharply. The mood in the hall dropped ten degrees.

"I didn't mean anything wrong," Mallory told her.

"No, I mean . . . trickster is an Indian term for . . . A trickster is a powerful person in a tribe. I'm sorry. It's just hearing you say it."

"What did you call your grandmother?"

"Grandmere?" Eden asked, her face lightening again. "It's French for 'Grandma.'"

"I know. I take French. But why would you call her that?"

"In Canada, a lot of Cree speak French."

"Is 'Cree' a French word?"

"Not really. It might be part of one. The Cree word for 'Cree' is *Iyniwok*."

"What do you mean, the Cree word for 'Cree'?"

"Well, Cree is the white . . . well, the European way of saying Cree, not the way we say it. *Iyniwok* just means 'the people.' Some people think it was short for Christienne, because so many Cree became Catholic . . . with the French priests, the voyageurs. But it's probably like a jumble of the two, like the word Chippewa is the English way to say Ojibway. It's just because that's how they understood it. They heard it that way. Ojibway. Chippewa."

"So the French trappers discovered the tribe?"

"Sure, we didn't exist before then."

"I don't mean that! I meant, no one ran into white people before the French came. I meant, you could take a boat and go a long way down the coast and not necessarily see any white people."

"Or other Indian people. I guess they thought they were the only people, or at least the only normal ones."

"Imagine how that was," Mally said. "You've got no car and no map, just a horse or a boat. One day, suddenly, you're like, 'Hey, there's a guy with white skin in a long black dress with a Bible!'"

"And another one with a gun," said Eden. "But a long time ago.

Let's go down now. You can leave your things. No one would ever take anything from my room. I want you to meet Cooper before the drumming. And you haven't lived until you've had my auntie's fry bread. Pure cholesterol."

When Mallory appeared, there was another round of exclamations and hugs. Eden's grandma, Annaisa, shyly accepted Mallory's thanks.

"You are a good friend to our daughter," she said simply, in a faded soft voice. Soon Mallory, who never spoke to anyone who didn't speak to her first, was chattering to all of the women. Some of the friends and family, whose Indian genes clearly were far up on the family tree, were pale with freckles. A few boys—she assumed these were the drummers or the dancers—wore long white shirts and leather leggings like Eden's dress.

The only person everyone treated just a bit differently was Eden.

Even the older women and men seemed almost to bow to her as she swept from group to group, laughing and teasing. Teasing, about everything from a boy's cowlick to a girl's new figure, seemed to be the favorite game.

But no one teased Eden. She was just a girl but there was something about her. She was like the hero in the tales Campbell read to them when they were little, but a girl.

Mally wanted to think it over, but the sights and voices in so many tones and languages swirled around her, mesmerizing her like a song. She settled herself on a blanket in one corner of the room where she could watch everyone together and had finished a plate of fry bread and venison when Eden came to find her.

"Mallory, this is Cooper, my brother," she told Mallory, who looked up and nearly dropped her plate. Cooper's wide white smile, the cheekbones that seemed to lift his face and deepen his eyes, were the same as Eden's. He wore the same pale clothing—was it deerskin? It was beaded in a design Mallory recognized as the constellation Ursa Major. Bear Clan. Atakahoop.

Star blanket.

"Hello," he said.

Could boys be beautiful? Mallory couldn't speak. She could hear Eden saying, *You'll know*.

COOPER

COOPER

W hat do you think of your first powwow?" Cooper asked.

I have to talk. He'll think I'm mentally challenged.

Mallory finally said, after ten seconds or more, "I honestly never ate such good food, and the dress . . ."

He said, "Grandmere has a way of knowing how to make a beautiful woman more beautiful."

"Mallory's not a flirt, Cooper," Eden scolded. "Don't make her feel all self-conscious."

"Are you coming to hear the drumming?" Cooper asked then. "It's our own circle. My cousin Ash started it. We call it Red Leaves. Very original."

"It's . . . great. It's a great name," Mallory said. "For a band."

"Someone has a crush," said Eden's sister Raina.

"Shush!" Eden said.

"Everyone loves Cooper!" Raina said. "He had to run to Boston to get away from the girls."

"My sisters talk a lot of nonsense," Cooper said.

"Mine too," Mallory told him.

"Eden says you have a twin."

"Yes, Meredith."

"But I bet your sister doesn't look like you tonight. Now I have to go to the drum."

Mallory had expected a band with different instruments, drums among them. Instead, six boys and young men, aged about sixteen to twenty-five, sat in a circle, each with a drum made of wood and leather, some decorated with ribbon, some polished but plain, some painted with bears. At a signal from Cooper's cousin, one of the young men gave a cry that startled Mallory with its tang of wild sweet mourning. Then all of the men joined in. There was a pattern to their cries and words, but it took time for Mallory to follow it. At first, all the words sounded like "Ay-ee, Ay-ee," but gradually she heard other words, words that sounded like "token-ah-ah-ah" and "bree-ah-toe-ah." The "Ay-ee" was the chorus, the part of the drumming that followed each stanza. When the last cry died away, there was a final thump of the drums.

"That was a song for the women, to ask them to bring the children up to be healthy and well," Eden explained. "This next one is a lullaby. It's about a baby who's afraid his father won't come home, but his mother is telling him the father has gone to find turtle shells and not to be afraid."

Raina and the other younger girls began to beg, "Dance, Coop. Do the Southern Dance."

"No way! I can't! I play hockey now!"

"Come on!" Raina cried.

"I forgot how!" Cooper said modestly.

"Come on," said the man called Ash. "It's wrong not to honor your family on the time of your birthday."

"Okay. Guilt always works. I'll give it a try."

Cooper began by trailing one arm before him as he swooped and turned. But quickly, the drumming increased in speed, and so did Cooper. His white boots, not like Eden's but cowboy boots with heels, kicked and slid in intricate patterns that repeated, each time with a new variation and a speed that went faster, then faster still. Cooper's two-step, one-step rhythm increased with it, and finally he leapt and whirled, ending with his clasped hands to his forehead.

The gathered crowd didn't applaud but cried out their approval. Cooper shook his head and walked away.

"I can't do it at all anymore," he told Eden.

"Now we'll dance," Eden said. "Come on." Mallory didn't think she could stand. She imagined what she felt about Cooper was like being drunk. "This is called the friendship dance. It's to welcome new wives and husbands, and new friends, like you."

"I can't do that."

"Oh, it's not like the men. It's like a line dance. See, two steps, two steps, one and two. Two steps, two steps, turn and one and two." To the slow beat, Mallory circled with Eden beside her and Eden's littlest sister, the one everyone called Honeybee, behind her. She was so busy concentrating on her feet that she didn't notice when Eden stepped into the center of the circle and with a sad, sweet smile on her face, swept her dress right and right, then left and left, reaching her hands up toward the stars, out toward the hills, and circling to encompass the ground. Mallory expected Eden's mother to beam with pride, but Wenona looked as though she might cry. Mally stepped back, out of the light, and backed right into Cooper.

"I'm sorry," she said. "Excuse me. I got caught up in watching Eden."

"She turns eighteen very soon. It's her time," Cooper said.

"Her time?"

"She . . . you know about Eden."

"I know some things."

"You know about the lion." Mallory tripped and Cooper caught her arm. A moment later, when he asked her to take a walk with him, she agreed without a word.

LAP BABY MOON

They walked along the edge of the woods. Campbell had always told Mallory to trust the voice inside her in any situation, and Mallory felt nothing but safety from Cooper, despite what he'd just said.

When they stopped, Cooper faced her. "I know you're close to Edensau. And so you know. My sister is in trouble. She loves a boy she can't marry."

The sweet smell of the pitch pine from the rows of silent trees that would fill the picture windows in Ridgeline and down in New Jersey and Manhattan was too intoxicating. Mallory couldn't get enough of it. She kept sneaking glances at Cooper, still resplendent in his white jacket and leggings, and forgetting that she was supposed to talk. Even the way he brushed back his hair, long enough in back almost to touch the upper part of his shoulders, was like part of his dance.

Finally, Mally shook herself and spoke up in Eden's defense. "I know she's too young. But someday? There are Indians here with red hair. Somebody must have married *somebody* who isn't all Cree."

"Little one. You don't get it. She can't marry anyone."

Mally stopped. They were almost out of earshot, the laughter and music of the powwow like the sound of a carnival far away. She stared up at Cooper. "She said that. I thought she was just mad at your parents. She didn't mean it literally."

"She did mean it. Mallory, my sister is our medicine woman."

"Big deal."

"It is a big deal. It's the biggest deal. Her life is to be here, to advise and teach and see, for all of us."

"How do you know?"

"What do you mean?" Cooper looked honestly puzzled.

"Did she get elected or something? Why not one of your other sisters? What do you have? Five?"

"She tells me what you see in your dreams."

"That's private!" Mallory told him.

"Not if it's about her. She's my sister," Cooper said. "What if it were your sister?"

"I see what you mean. But . . . she tells you what I dream? About the . . ."

"The lion, yes," Cooper said.

"This is way too serious a talk for two people who met fifteen minutes ago. And I wasn't ready," Mally said.

"I know. I'm sorry. But there's no one else on earth I can talk to about it who won't just say, 'Oh well, it's the law.' And it's getting to me. The lion is . . . is . . ."

"Don't," Mallory told him. "Just don't."

"Eden is the shape-shifter. She's the one with the power. She was born that way. It's her gift."

"She told me about shape-shifting. She said it was an old myth."

"It's not," Cooper told her gently. "It's real. It's her gift."

"Not to her! I bet not to her! I have a gift too, and it's no gift!"

"What?"

"Nothing," Mallory said bitterly. "What's a shape-shifter?"

With one hand, Cooper indicated a place where they could sit. It was an old fire pit, surrounded on four sides by split-log seats. With a branch, Cooper swept one of the seats clean. Just one. Mallory had no choice but to sit down at his side. She could feel the heat of his arm next to hers.

After a moment of perusing the sky, Cooper said, "It'll rain tomorrow. It's already getting cool. We're lucky it didn't come tonight."

Mallory shifted to face him. "We weren't talking about the weather."

Cooper answered, "I know. But I don't want to talk about it any more than you want to hear about it." He paused. "It's enough to enjoy a beautiful night with a pretty girl when all you do is spend all your time cramped up in a dorm studying." Mallory's chest was still thrumming from his description of her as a pretty girl when Cooper said, "You know what a shape-shifter is."

"No, I don't."

"If you don't, then you won't believe me."

"Trust me," Mallory said. "I'll believe it. I could tell you things . . ."

"You could?" Cooper stood up. He studied the rising moon with its cloak of misty cloud over Mallory's head. Then he sat back down, carefully taking one of Mally's hands and holding it lightly in both of his. "Really? I thought there weren't many others like us."

"Like you . . . what?"

"You know . . . things regular people wouldn't believe."

"Try me."

Cooper looked hard at Mallory. "At the full moon, Eden changes, for three days, into her totem. And her totem animal . . ."

"It's the lion."

"Yes, Mallory. It's our guide, our spirit animal."

"And mine," Mally said dully.

"Yours?"

"She led me to see that a girl was going to be badly hurt. She probably saved my sister's life last year. She's probably been watching me since I was a child, or so it seems. I guess I was assigned to her by the stars. That's probably the only reason she's my friend."

"She's your friend because you make her laugh."

Mallory smiled and said, "She said that? I don't make most people laugh."

"No?"

"My sister says I'm the world's biggest social zero. But I think most things kids do are dumb."

"So do I."

Both of them stood then. It seemed natural for Cooper to go on holding Mallory's hand as they walked in silence for another few minutes toward the thick dark line of the trees. At last, Mallory said, "And I don't do as much as other kids either, because of my *gift*. It wears me out."

"Tell me about it."

Mally said, "You wouldn't believe *me*."

Cooper smiled and reached out, hesitated for just a second, and then stroked Mally's hair. "I see another reason you're close to my sister. You have hair like Eden. You must be sisters in the spirit way."

"Maybe," Mallory said briefly, electrically aware that a boy was touching her, like a girl, for the first time. "So why can't this just leave her alone?"

"Eden doesn't want it, that's for sure," Cooper admitted.

"I don't blame her," Mallory cried, near to tears. "I don't want what I have either. That's why Eden missed the year of school. It wasn't because of your little sister's birth."

"No, she had to take a year for her instruction and be with the women, the aunts from Canada and all over the country."

Mally said, "Cooper. She doesn't just not *want* it. She's furious."

"That's why we're talking about it."

"No. It's more than the gift itself. She thinks people at school believe she was left back. She doesn't say it was because your mother was sick after Tanisi was born." Tanisi was Eden's three-year-old sister, who was born when Mrs. Cardinal was over forty. Mallory knew it was more dangerous for women that age; her mother always said so.

"She was sick, my mother, but part of the way that my sister helped her . . ."

"Was Indian superpowers?"

"Yes," Cooper said. "Eden learned the words and motions. She made her own ceremonial clothing. She learned the prayers and the . . . things I don't even know. She used the herbs for healing the spirit. She learned when she would change and how, and where to go when she did."

"And lost a year of her life! Why didn't she tell me the truth?" Mally asked. She looked back at the longhouse, listening to the laughter and the music, the joyful cries as more and more people arrived. All of it seemed false now, like a big, unkind joke on Eden.

Cooper asked, "How could she take a chance? She had to wonder. Would you still be her friend? Would you be scared?"

"No. My twin and I . . ."

"That's right. You're a twin. Of course. Eden writes about your sister too. That's powerful medicine."

"Whatever it is, it's apparently part of our package. We can't get rid of it. But I hate that this has to happen to Eden. She's my . . . best friend."

"She's my best sister. I don't like it much either. Are you cold? Do you want my vest?" Cooper asked. "You shivered."

Mallory did want his vest, but with him inside it. She pushed the thought away and said, "I shivered but not because of the temperature of the air. It's because, well, I already knew. I . . . can tell. Like intuition."

Cooper said softly, "It's more than that."

"Yes. It's more than that."

"Eden is scared for you. And your sister. It's a huge thing, having to know."

"You bet it is," said Mallory. "Every day, I wish I would wake up cured. If I had a . . . I don't know what . . . a light sword or a wand and I could just banish the bad things . . . but I can't. We can't. We have to be this way our whole lives. I'm afraid too. I'm afraid for Eden."

"About James."

"I know she's dangerous to James. I don't know how."

"I don't either. I know he threatens our clan. But if he saw her change, it would be bad."

"Bad luck?" Mallory asked.

"No," Cooper said slowly, his hand on Mally's shoulder. "She would have to kill him."

LOOK BOTH WAYS

LOOK BOTH WAYS

Are you nuts?" Mallory measured the distance from where she and Cooper stood to the longhouse. She hadn't felt this way since she and Merry faced David the first time in the deserted building site—where he threatened to break their arms or worse. Drew wouldn't come barreling along to save her now. And then Mally measured her emotions, as Campbell had taught her, this time separating out her attraction to Cooper, which she couldn't deny was making her breath come faster, against the fear his words kindled.

Cooper stood an appropriate distance from her, motionless. What he said about Eden, he said with infinite grief. Mally relaxed. "Kill James? I knew it was bad, but not this bad."

"The shape-changer has to kill whoever might see her change shape. It's the law."

"I've heard all about *the law*! At least mine," Mally snapped. "And I think it's bullshit, personally."

"She has to, or the whole tribe is betrayed. We lose our medicine. We lose our power."

"Power to what? Why should she give up her life for you guys?"

"Mallory, years ago, my auntie Abulay ran away. She gave up the power. And so we fell. The men died at sea. The fish didn't come. We moved here from Canada, my mother and father and her sisters who were left. We started over. My older sister, Bly, is studying to be a doctor at Johns Hopkins. My brother Rayner is in law school. The kids will change the lives we live. That's because of Eden's medicine."

"That's because Bly's a . . . person of color and so's Rayner and they're smart! Does Eden get to go to college? Does she have to take a week off at semester break to change into a puma? How can you believe this is anything but a coincidence?"

"How can you not? If Eden marries, there has to be a whole other generation after her before another medicine woman is born. Maybe more. You don't get to choose, Mallory. You know that yourself." Cooper's voice was infinitely gentle. She could smell him as he stood closer to her, a spicy smell like smoke and peppers. "I have to leave and go back in a week. You need to help her. My sister has a rebellious heart. She could run away."

"You ran away!" Mally cried out.

"I went to school!" Cooper pleaded.

"But you didn't want to see her suffer?"

"It was school. That was what was expected of me."

"I never knew you when you lived here."

"I know people you know. I know your boyfriend, Drew."

Mally smiled. "Drew's my buddy, not my boyfriend." She thought of her house, its warm orange squares of windows alight. Her bed under the eaves, her old bear. It seemed so impossibly far from where she stood.

Suddenly Mallory realized a fact that made her heart stammer. "So this weekend . . . the moon was nearly full a few days ago."

"Yes. This is her time."

"It's not right."

"Would your sister say that? She's protected people who were going to be hurt—like the girl you know. Maybe others we don't know about. The shape-shifter is a trickster too. She can lead evil people astray. Hunters who see her will not have good luck. No one is supposed to see her when she's in her shape. But if someone sees her when she shifts, then that person has to die or Edensau has to . . ."

"Has to what?"

"She has to do what I said before."

"Or else?"

"Or else . . . stay in the form of a mountain lion forever. She could still do her medicine. But she couldn't be a human being again, ever. She'd be in danger every day. Hunters. Hikers. Sometime, she'd be caught, hurt."

"Not to mention having to spend her whole life eating rabbits and sleeping on the floor of a cave!" Mallory snapped at him.

It all sounded so familiar.

Mallory's own parents couldn't know about her and Merry.

No one could know about her and Merry, except Grandma and

Drew and now this strange stranger of a boy. This boy with the strong chin and the straight shoulders, the muscled forearms and gentle hands.

Tonight had been enchanted. And it was turning into a sad parallel to her own messed-up existence. One part of her was feeling things she had never felt, wondering if Cooper had summers at home and what he'd do when he graduated. And the same boy was telling her that her best friend might have to eat an innocent jogger who happened to come along at the wrong moment.

Why did anyone have to be "gifted"? Why did people ever complain about ordinary lives? She heard Grandma Gwenny's voice in her head.

Her grandmother told them, *You do good. You can change lives. You can be like Saint Bridget the Brave, and change lives.*

There was a purpose. There was a purpose for people like her and Merry and Eden. At least now she could talk to Eden. For this, she was grateful to Cooper. She was grateful too, for his beauty and the way he danced and sang, for making her feel like a woman for the first time.

She looked up at him. "Cooper, I promise to do my best to protect her and to make sure she doesn't do anything stupid over James, if I can."

Cooper put one finger on Mally's cheek. "I'll always be thankful that I met you here tonight. I hope it's not the last time I see you." He stopped. "You're so little. Are you really only twelve or something? Are you lying about going to school with my sister?"

Mallory laughed. He was only teasing, flirting. It was like an actual taste on her tongue, an indescribably sweet taste, to play this kind of game with a cute guy. "If I'm lying, so is Eden!"

"Look at the moon, Mallory. The cloud ring broke away for a moment. It's an optical illusion, but it looks as though there are two moons, a big moon holding a little one. We call it the Lap Baby Moon. It's lucky to see it."

"I feel lucky I came. Despite everything."

He kissed her then. Although it was her first kiss, clearly it wasn't Cooper's. When she moved her mouth, he found it again, and drew her closer, putting his arms around her in a way that didn't feel gross but so that he was nearly lifting her off her feet.

Which was lucky.

Otherwise Mallory would have ended up in a heap on the ground. Her whole body disappeared into a little column of light that flowed from her lips—the only thing she could feel. Despite having spent her life in the company of a brain that never stopped, Mallory passed ninety seconds without a thought in her head.

Later, as she and Eden lay side by side in their sleeping bags watching the dawn come up, Mallory told Eden what she and Cooper had talked about.

"I thought you would," Eden said. "I'm glad you know. I even knew he was the guy for you. But I won't do it, Mally. I've done it long enough."

"You have no choice, Edie. Like us," Mallory whispered. "I can't imagine how it must hurt. I really can't. I don't know what it's like to be in love. But for you, Eden, it's not just letting people down. It's dangerous for you, you personally, to break the tradition."

"I don't care. There's nothing that is so wonderful as being in love. Or so terrible."

And Mallory couldn't begin to disagree.

THE INTRUDER

THE INTRUDER

To audition people she might want for friends—at least according to Erika—Neely invited the whole freshman class to a Halloween party. For good measure, she added twenty sophomores and juniors.

It didn't matter that Halloween was over.

"Anyone could have a Halloween party on Halloween," Neely said. "I want this to be more than a Halloween party. I think I want it to be a pagan festival."

Meredith couldn't imagine what that meant, but she knew she didn't want to miss it.

"Come with," she told Mallory. "What, do you have a blood disease or something? I've never seen you so lazy and you're always lazy."

"I have stuff on my mind," Mallory said. "And I wouldn't go to a party at Neely Chaplin's for money."

"Then you don't really want to find out," Merry said.

"Find out . . ."

"Who's planning to hurt someone next at the tryout. You know, they're on Monday. I never really got an answer that night."

Mallory sighed. She was restless. Life seemed to be both boring and a constant source of distress, like a broken heater that made more noise than warmth. Even soccer wasn't much fun. Since Cooper, even moonlight or the smell of burning leaves was a sort of sweet torment.

He had sent her a letter, which she received before he even left Ridgeline.

> *Dear Mallory,*
>
> *I'm so happy I met you. And I'm so grateful you're there for Eden. I wish you weren't really twelve! Just kidding. Remember the Lap Baby Moon. I'll be thinking about you.*
>
> *Your friend,*
>
> *Cooper Cardinal*

Mally kept the letter in a slit she'd cut in the lining of her backpack and thought she should probably have it laminated so it didn't fall apart from her taking it out and reading it four times a day. "Your friend." It didn't exactly say, *I'm so grateful I met you. Please wait ten years and marry me.* But how could it? They'd spent all of thirty minutes together. The fact that she could think of nothing else . . . "It's just biology!" her mother would say. The other thing about Cooper that made Mallory happy was that her mother and Merry didn't know anything about him.

Campbell admired the black dress and black moccasins, stroking them and marveling at the intricacy. Aunt Kate even wondered aloud if Eden's grandmother might give a lesson in beading at the community center while Mallory prayed, *Oh no, oh please no,* until Campbell finally said it was a craft that was probably too time-consuming for most people. Campbell packed the dress between layers of tissue carefully, so that Mallory could wear it again and keep it always. Mallory wore the moccasins all the time. Eden had told her they were made never to wear out, that her people had walked all the way from Canada in shoes just like these.

Neely's party would at least distract her from reliving every second of her first kiss—ten times a day.

She said, "Fine. I'll go as an idiot. I am anyway."

"What's wrong with you, Mally? Same old?"

"Something new." Meredith's eyes lit up. "And private," Mally added firmly. Merry purred. She was no fool. But she didn't press Mallory for details.

Because it might be fun, and lead to more opportunities for overhearing other people's plots, the twins decided to dress identically, so that they could change personalities at will—like shape-shifters, Mallory thought. Two years earlier, their parents had gone to a party dressed up as a pair of Aces. The cards were so nicely made by the twins' aunt Kate, the Craft Queen, that all they needed was to be dusted off. The hoods (which looked to Mallory, who had recently become interested in Lady Jane Gray, like executioners' hoods) were in perfect shape and clean, in a plastic bag. All the girls had to do was pull on wool tights and turtlenecks and the black suede boots their parents had given them the previous Christmas.

Mally was curious about the shoe-tape issue.

But she figured that, given what had happened to Crystal, all of the girls trying out would be checking their shoes in any case. She went along for a reason that she didn't share with her twin. Hanging out with Dad and watching the game or practicing with Adam just didn't cut it anymore. She wouldn't admit it, but she was tired of lying around brooding or being a freshman who acted like she was still in sixth grade.

Just one taste of a new life was enough to make her old life boring. Sometimes, Mallory wished she'd never had it.

Neely's party was held on her front lawn in a heated tent, so it didn't matter that it was November. Campbell dropped all of the girls off at the end of the driveway, where the reliable Stuart was waiting to ferry them to the top. Surprisingly, Kim Jellico had called, at the last minute, and asked to come along—for one night deserting the friends from Deptford Consolidated she usually hung with now. Crystal, still on crutches, sent melodramatic texts every fifteen minutes, requesting cell-phone photos. Alli was dressed as a harem girl. Erika wore an old suit and a slouchy hat to look like a mobster. Kim was wearing a Dallas Cowboy cheerleader's sort of outfit—basically a bikini with a cowboy hat and silver boots.

Though she had lost weight and gained height since David's death, Kim was still a big and broad-shouldered girl, and the two-piece, with its little bolero, looked to Campbell like a few pieces of tinsel on a Christmas tree. She wondered why Dave or Bonnie hadn't made Kim wear a body stocking underneath. But Bonnie had gone into what seemed to Campbell to be a permanent middle distance since David died. She did her work competently, but no longer went to yoga or the book club. Not for the first time, Campbell thought that she and her daughter Merry had both lost their best friends when David died. The tragedy was far from over. Kim wouldn't even be fifteen until December. She was still a kid, but so closed. Maybe being with Merry would do her good.

"Have a good time, Kimmie!" Campbell called impulsively. Kim turned and waved, and the smile that crossed her face was brief as a passing cloud.

The girls couldn't begin to count the windows, each with a different backlit Halloween silhouette. A projector scrolled flying bats across the facade and blue lights seemed to erupt periodically from the roof. Costumed adults, dressed as ghouls and pale alluring vampires, stepped from behind trees to beckon them. There was a life-size guillotine. But when they saw that it dispensed Toblerone bars when the "blade" dropped, everyone felt better. Will Brent started filling his pockets.

Neely greeted them in a see-through chiffon cape over a bodysuit threaded with twinkle lights. Her hair was swept up in curls, similarly arrayed and electrified. A few of the guys arrived at the same time as the twins and their friends.

"What are you supposed to be?" Will Brent asked Neely. "An electric eel?"

"Ha. Ha. Ha," Neely said. "I'm actually dressed as Night. Just

Night."

"She could be an ad for outlet covers," Mallory said.

"Shut up and be nice," Merry whispered.

"At least they have cheese and tomato sandwiches," Kyle Karzniak put in. "Jalapeno poppers too. Ginger ale and orange juice?"

"Fake mimosas," said Caitlin, taking one off a tray. She winked at Merry. "Wonder where the real ones are." Merry put her finger to her lips.

A deejay was setting up. The whole tent had a temporary planked floor, sprinkled with bushels of glittery little moons and stars.

The cheerleaders and Mallory huddled and surveyed the crowd.

Neely, after greeting a fleet of guests, floated over to them. Suddenly, she asked, "Are you guys twins?"

"Just good friends," Mallory answered.

"Did I know that and just forget? How could I have gone through two months of school without noticing?" Neely asked herself.

"Do you notice much?" Mallory asked.

"Don't be ridiculous," Neely said. "I see everything that counts." She whirled away for a moment and waved to a group of older boys. "Like that." She pretended to touch her finger to a hot stove and then to her tongue.

"That's Drew!" Merry said. "Who invited Drew?"

"He's cute," Neely said. "He's looking at Kim. Hey, Kim, he's noticing you! He must like girls with a little meat on their bones."

Kim whirled and stalked away from the group to join a knot of kids at the other end, mostly boys that included Dane Greenberg. All of them looked approvingly at her boy-kini.

"What's with her?" Neely asked. "She must be a mount. They're all biggies. She's got nice legs but that rear end is a little too much for those boy shorts, huh?"

"Neely, she's sensitive about that," Merry said softly. "And it's not just that. Her brother just died. You should take it easy. Since then, she hasn't come out with us much."

"I'm sorry," Neely said. "She's always giving me the evil eye."

"Maybe she's jealous that you fit in and she . . . doesn't," Merry said, realizing at this moment that what she said was true and it was as much her fault as anyone's. She hadn't called Kim in months. Why didn't she go after Kim now? Kim had come only because of Merry. Why didn't she get her butt over and talk to Kim and lead her back? It was because Kim was . . . strange now. Kim was loud and too sexy and weird, and Meredith didn't really want to be seen with her. Truth was, she was ashamed of her old friend and how she was practically Velcro'ed to Dane. To cover her own unkindness, Merry said, "Kim's probably lonely now. We should all be nice to her. And Neely, you're like two people. You're nice when it's just you, but in front of a bunch of people, it's like you change."

"Speaking of cheerleading," Neely said, interrupting Merry, "we could do things with that twin business you guys have going on. Did you ever consider cheering, Mallory?"

"I have, but I decided I'd rather be boiled," Mallory said.

The other girls looked from one to the other. They knew the person speaking had to be Mallory, or were the twins goofing around? The girls had removed the single garnet Merry wore in her right ear and Mally in her left that had been placed there the day after they were born, so that their parents could tell them apart.

Just then Drew ambled by.

"Brynn, which one of you is you?" he asked.

"Me," Merry said, laughing.

"No, come on! You can't be Mallory. You're in too good a mood," Drew said.

"I really am Mallory, Drewsky," Merry teased him.

"And hey, I'm in a good mood," Neely offered, taking Drew's arm. Drew looked at her as though she had some kind of rash and politely patted her hand as he removed it. Neely shrugged. "Your loss! Anyhow, I was thinking, my mom could help. She still has the style and the moves. No offense to your coach but she's kind of old school. Or anyway, old. Anyhow. My mom is only thirty-six. She started cheering for the Rams in college, and then she got an MBA in marketing and she runs her own business with cruelty-free beauty products, vegan hats, and jewelry."

"VEGAN hats?" Drew asked. "You mean, like a lettuce ball cap? Or a mushroom fedora? And your mom was . . . what?"

"Silly," Neely said, obviously flirting. "She was a professional cheerleader. An Embraceable Ewe."

"A what? A You?"

"A Ewe, a St. Louis Rams cheerleader. Years ago. But the hats. They're called vegan because they're not made with any leather. They're natural products."

"You've obviously never heard a carrot scream," Drew said.

"Stop!" Neely went on, laughing. "She runs the business out of the house. You could see her on the shopping channel if you wanted. What I mean is, she has her own schedule. She could help out, give us that snap we really need."

"I'd watch the shopping channel," Mally said, "if I lost half my brain."

"Brynn, now I know that's you," Drew said.

"And why do we need snap?" Caitlin asked. "Neely, you aren't even on the team yet."

"Not until Monday," Neely said.

"Or ever," Mallory added.

"How can you be Merry's identical twin?" Neely asked. "She was so nice at my house, even when she had the nightmare."

"Don't pay any attention to Mallory," Merry said. "She really has lost half her brain. She's a soap opera addict."

"Wait! I love soap operas. I never miss *General Hospital*. I record it," Neely said.

"See? You're soul sisters," Merry told her twin.

"I'm sorry, Neely. Anyone who loves Erica Kane can't be all bad," Mallory said. "In fact, you remind me of her. Did you say nightmare? What nightmare was this?"

"Never mind," Merry said.

"I don't mind. You can have all the nightmares you want. But I have a strange feeling about this one."

"You're being paranoid," Merry told Mally.

"She's just defensive. Lots of fringe-y girls get defensive," Neely put in, with a huge dramatic sigh. Drew turned away in disgust.

"Fringe-y? What do you mean by that?" Mallory asked.

"On the fringe," Neely said. "Of things."

"I'm not . . ." Mallory began and then noticed that her sister was trying to slip away with Alli. She turned her big cardboard Ace sideways to block Merry. "What nightmare? Was it scary? Like . . . that?"

"It wasn't. Or I would have told you. Just weird," Meredith whispered.

"What was it about?"

"It was about the lion."

"About the lion? Merry! And you didn't tell me?"

"I wasn't scared. How could it *hurt anyone* if it's a symbol?" Merry was impatient. "We agreed it wasn't a real lion."

"What was it doing?"

"Well, you were running and it was following you, up on the ridge trail by our camp. And the strange part was, it was summer. At first, I thought it was hunting you, until I had this bizarre feeling."

Mallory felt her eyes brim. Last summer. Eden would have been watching out for her, making sure no one else hurt her. Eden, her guardian.

"It wasn't hunting me," she told Merry softly.

"The feeling I had was . . . well . . . I couldn't really describe it until now."

"What?" Mallory asked.

"I felt that I knew the lion. Personally. Like you said."

Mallory said, "You do."

"And then I saw it stop and lie down. It was looking down on a campsite. There was a guy with a red sleeping bag and a BoSox cap. It just watched him." Mallory sighed and then nodded as Merry went on, "I'm sure there's an explanation. But I have to hear about this right now?"

"No. Not tonight. Tonight, we'll just be regular kids," Mally said.

Merry answered, "As if."

THE EVIDENCE

THE EVIDENCE

By Monday morning, despite a long shampoo, Mallory still had glitter in her hair. As she brushed through her hair before school, she remembered how invisible hands had released a shower of stars from the trees at Neely's house at 10:30 P.M., signaling to everyone, including the few couples cuddling up in the rock garden (Kim and Dane among them), it was time to go home.

The party hadn't been much fun.

But the long evening with Neely at her mini-mansion was enough to convince Mally: The tape came from her fancy stuck-up little paws.

Neely was a spoiled little brat, despite her weakness for *General Hospital*. She would do anything to bring a little pizzazz to the poor Ridgeline line—including enlisting her mom—and she talked like making one of the two varsity spots was a foregone conclusion. She was surer of herself than Mallory's own conceited older sister (well, Merry was older, by two minutes!). Neely was planning the same thing—or something like it—for the tryouts today. She had to be. Merry had seen the beringed hands in her dream. Who else would have them?

A note would prompt Coach Everson to sit the girls down and question them, in that way adults had of breaking kids down. Confession. Suspension. Expulsion.

Relaxation.

A vision with an easy fix!

Neely would go to the Catholic school that billed itself as the area's only "genuine prep school." All rich delinquents went there. It would serve her right—the little ewe.

Merry had finally promised to deliver the note, even though she was worried about everything from hidden cameras to fingerprints.

So, happily, Mallory set out for her jog, wondering if a lean pale shape would slip along beside her among the scrub trees as she trod the path up the ridge. Cooper had flown back to Boston. But Mallory had woken sure that she could save Eden—even from herself. Her heart pounded, and she felt its strength blooming, a warmth throughout her. She and Cooper, in on this together, would stop Eden from her plan to give up her destiny. And then she and Eden, together, would find their way out of her destined prison.

Edie would have a normal life. One of the two of them would have that. There had to be a way.

She would make this gift of hers do some work *for* her.

Mallory picked up her stride.

Back at home, Merry nestled down into her quilts. The morning was chilly and she needed all her rest for tryouts. Tryouts were today. . . . She wasn't even tense. There was no reason to get up early. Merry's bed was angled toward the door so that she could survey the array of outfits she'd laid out the night before, to choose from in the morning, without even getting up. She planned on the luxury of another half hour of drowsing.

Then Merry sat up and whammed her head so hard she saw double. Reaching up, she felt for blood. How? She looked down at her comforters, in a tangle around her feet. She'd clearly scrooched herself around in bed until her head was facing the footboard, the way she used to do when she'd sneak into bed with Mallory! But she hadn't done that for years.

Why now?

Then she heard the voices downstairs. Way downstairs, on the first floor. These were what had wakened her. They were familiar—they were her parents. They were having a fight, and making no effort to cover it up.

This was interesting, in a creepy way.

So was her head!

The first tryout she'd had to go to school looking like a refugee from the burn ward, and now she'd have a lump on her head the size of a fist! Great! How could this happen in her one life?

"You're scaring them with the way you're acting," Tim said, in a voice so harsh Merry could hardly recognize it. Normally, the Brynns (quite proudly) explained that, despite their low-level sarcasm and minor bickering, if one of them was really mad, the angry one had to go outside and walk it off. But no one was walking it off now. "You're acting weird and it's time you told them why, Campbell."

"Tim, you know they'll hate me for it," their mother said.

"You should have thought of that back in July when you decided!"

"When I decided! I wasn't the only one, as I recall!" Campbell said. "I think both of us agreed that night up at the camp!"

"I didn't think you'd moan and complain and snipe at everyone every day because of it. I thought this was what you wanted."

Campbell said, "I'm sorry, Tim. I'd love to go on talking nonsense with you but I have to go try to keep some people from dying."

"Right. We lowly merchants stand in awe of you professional folks," Merry's father said.

Merry came around the corner of the landing and saw Tim and Campbell, face-to-face in the kitchen. Tim was looking down at her mother as if he really wanted to get in her face, and Campbell, fierce as a terrier, wasn't about to back off. As Tim turned to stomp away, he saw Merry.

Merry smiled at her father.

"I hit my head," Merry said.

"You hit your *head*?" Campbell asked. "How did you do that?"

"I hit it on the ceiling. I turned around so my head was at the bottom of the bed, by the window."

"Just like you used to do when you were little," Tim said. He pulled Meredith up into a hug but she stiffened in his arms. "Listen, Merry Heart, you overheard your mom and me . . ."

"I don't want to know!" Merry said, struggling. "I don't want to know about you guys' stuff."

"Well, we were just being jerks," Campbell told her. "It's no big deal."

"Are you getting a divorce?"

"Getting a divorce?" Tim was flabbergasted. "No one's getting a divorce."

"Well, you were so absorbed in fighting you didn't even hear me yell! I practically got knocked out!" said Merry. "Before, I had the flaky skin. Now I'm going to have a huge bruise!"

"Do you have more of that makeup?" Campbell asked, pressing an ice pack to Merry's head.

"Yes."

"If you get a bruise, that should cover it up. No one will see it on the stage. Are you dizzy? Do you think you have a concussion?"

Merry said, "MOM."

"Well, take some ibuprofen for the swelling," Campbell told her. "And keep that ice on."

"Okay," Merry said. Slowly, she went back up to her room. Just then, Mallory banged in the door and rushed up the stairs, two at a time. She stopped in the door frame of their room. "What's wrong? You usually have four outfits out by now."

"Mom and Dad had this huge fight."

"Merry, what's that on your head? You're not saying that they hit you?"

"As a matter of fact, I hit my head."

"How?"

"I turned around in my bed."

"Like I did that other time?"

"Like that exactly."

"That's so weird."

"But it wasn't because of a dream. It must have been because I heard them fighting . . . subconsciously."

"Well, I'm sorry you got that . . . Wow, that's some egg, Merry!"

"Thanks, Mal!"

"But that explains it. You've got a concussion. Mom and Dad would never get divorced."

"You didn't hear them," Merry wailed.

"They're not the divorce type," said Mallory. "Don't you want to do some splits or something? Warm up? Change the subject?"

"You didn't hear them!"

"Are you nuts?" Mallory asked Merry. "Don't answer. You are nuts. They so wouldn't get a divorce."

"How do you know? How do you really know about anything? Did you think David Jellico was a killer?"

"Yes, I did, in fact. It was you who wanted to marry him." Mallory added, "Merry, take it easy. It's because Mom is a boss now like Dad, and they have nervous tension times two. Mom doesn't like being an administrator. I wish she'd go back to her old job. You know, there is something going on. Maybe Mom is sick. She's being too nice one minute and too crabby the next minute. She's yelling at us to pick up lint on the carpet at night and the next day, she walks right past the room without yelling at us to make the beds. Maybe Dad, like, gambled a bunch of money away or something."

Merry snorted. "Dad? Gambling? Now you're hallucinating. Dad won't spend a dollar on the $179 million Power Ball."

They both heard Drew laying on the horn.

"I haven't got my makeup on!" Merry cried.

"You may have noticed, you haven't got your clothes on either. And I haven't even had a shower," said Mallory. "But it doesn't matter. I have gym second hour." Mallory pulled up the window and yelled, "Drewsky! Go ahead. We will grab a ride with my dad! The little princess doesn't have her game face on yet! Tryouts today!"

Fifteen minutes later, Mallory had ducked in and out of the shower, and Meredith, with shaking hands, applied her "no-makeup makeup." Even though it was tryouts day, she was so rattled that she pulled on the first white shirt she found in the closet over her jeans.

When they came down, Tim was zipping his windbreaker.

"We need a ride," Mallory announced.

"You need a ride, what?" Tim asked.

"We need a ride to *school*," Merry said. "Things were so nuts here this morning Drew had to leave without us."

"You need a ride . . . please," Tim said.

"Well, please, of course," said Mallory. "And thanks for telling us you were about to break up or something. You made her smack her head!"

Tim looked at them. He thought they were kidding. "She smacked her own head!"

"Why'd you build the room like a danger pit?"

"Mallory, most people don't spin around in their beds while they're asleep!"

"Most people aren't in danger of losing IQ points if they do! Your room is the size of the YMCA in Deptford. We can barely fit in ours!"

"That's enough from you, young lady!"

"Fine!" Mallory snapped. She glanced up at her dad. "I'm sorry. I was rude."

"Apology accepted. Mally and Meredith, your mom and I have had fights before, and you didn't even notice. All parents have arguments. Listen, get in the car. We'll talk on the way. Even though I'm not saving lives like Campbell, I do have a business to run. I'm going to be late."

In the car, Mallory asked, "So what's going on, Dad?"

Tim wondered if the twins had some weird hormonal condition Campbell would know about. Or maybe, as he'd told his wife, they really did sense what was going on. "Mom's been a little off her feed," Tim admitted. "She hasn't been feeling well. She's tired."

"Off her feed? You mean, she won't eat?" *I told you she had an ulcer*, Mally thought, extra loudly, to her sister, who nodded. "She eats! Crazy stuff like tea and chocolate milk shakes and steak sauce on salad! You keep making these vague statements, and it's like she has cancer and you won't tell us."

"She's just got a little bug," Tim said cheerfully. "I said that."

"Months ago! Flu doesn't last that long, Dad," Meredith said.

He doesn't even care, Mally thought. Thank God it wasn't *him*. Every time her father had a cough, he treated it like it was leukemia.

"Dad, would you tell us if anything was really wrong?" Mally asked. "We need a really stable life right now."

"Of course. Look, things are fine. Don't worry, Mally. Merry, I'm sorry we argued in front of you, though, technically, you eavesdropped."

Tim leaned over and gave each of them a kiss. "Good luck today at tryouts, Mer. By the way, Kim called you last night. I left a note under your door."

"I didn't see it because I was unconscious, Dad. Sorry."

Tim made a huffing sound.

They headed into school. Suddenly, Merry put both hands on Mallory's shoulders. "Stop for a second," she said.

"What's wrong?" Mally asked.

"Maybe I did hurt my head. I was dizzy there for a minute. I'm fine now. It just *hurts* like crazy!"

"Are you sure you weren't . . . passing out?"

"No," Merry said. "Really fine, Ster!"

But it was Kim's name that had done it, brought back what had really spun her around like a top in the bed before she ever heard her parents bickering. She'd dreamed of Kim, in a place that was nowhere that Merry recognized—somewhere outside in the dark with two guys, one with long dirty ropes of hair, one with no hair at all—her Halloween costume top ripped, her makeup smeared, staggering while the guys held her up, pretending to laugh.

But Kim wasn't laughing. She was crying. Hard.

She had called Merry before this happened. But when?

SECOND TRY

SECOND TRY

How could someone who looked just like you be as hard to find as a needle in a haystack?

There were five minutes left before sixth hour and Mallory was searching the lunchroom frantically for Merry. She'd already combed the gym and the library. Merry had to be somewhere!

Finally, she spotted her.

Calm down, Mallory told herself. *It's going to be fine.* As long as Merry had talked to Coach Everson, or left a note, all would be well. None of it will happen. Mallory tried to drag her tense shoulders down from around her ears. How could she have believed anything would ever be simple that involved them?

"Merry!" she called. "Wait up! I have to talk to you."

"What?" Merry replied impatiently. "I've got a vocab quiz in French in five minutes. And then I have to concentrate and be centered. Can't it wait?"

"No, it can't. I have to be sure you left Coach Everson a note about how somebody might try to hurt somebody again at tryouts. You did, right?"

"No," Merry said.

"Meredith! But I told you to!"

"And I thought about it. I decided that nobody would be stupid enough to try anything like that twice no matter what I saw in my dream."

"But you saw it yourself!"

"It was just a warning."

"No, it wasn't. It was real."

"Well, I think it was a warning. I have a brain."

"That's where you're wrong," Mallory said. "Listen. You can't be limp about this. You promised you'd tell Coach Everson. You lied to me!"

"You're overreacting, Mal. If I really thought there was a danger, don't you think I'd have left her a note?"

"There really is a danger! You have to get in touch with her! Why don't you get this?"

"Because I am not listening to you," Merry said. She shifted her backpack and opened her voluminous yellow purse, pulling out a blue-and-brown scarf. She twisted it and made the "New York knot" around her neck. Merry's scarf didn't coordinate with anything she had on, except her big rubber jelly purse. Without meaning to, Mallory made a quizzical face.

"I'm updating my look," said Merry. "Matchy-matchy is out. Your shoes aren't supposed to go with your jewelry."

"Thank heaven you told me," Mallory said. "I was about to put on the wrong scarf myself. Listen, dumb girl, we don't have time to talk about scarves. You have to listen. I have a strong feeling. Something really, really, really bad is going to happen unless you fix it. I counted on you."

"Well, if you're so sure, and you can't count on little old me, you do it, then." Merry slammed the door of her locker closed, which went unnoticed because of the flurry of activity, kids throwing away their yogurt containers and half-finished sandwiches and rushing to class. "If I talk to her, she'll think I'm in on it."

"Why? What about a note?"

"She'd know my handwriting! I can't take that chance."

"That's what you really care about, Meredith. YOU! So it's okay with you if somebody ends up in a coma?"

"What do you mean?"

"Meredith," she said quietly. "I had a dream that was real."

"And when did you have it?"

"Last hour."

"You had study hall last hour."

Mallory asked, "What do you do in study hall?" Meredith's cheeks flushed. "Okay, well, sometimes I sleep too. And I saw. Meredith. Some. One. Is. Going. To. Get. Hurt. And this time it won't be a ligament. I saw the ambulance lights. I saw a person on a stretcher in the Ridgeline uniform. Do you want something bad to happen to Alli or Erika or Caitlin or Kim?"

Merry paled. "If you're such a real life-changing psychic, go do some wonder work, wonder girl."

"Why are you so hostile?" Mallory shouted. This time heads did turn, and the whole south hall went quiet. Mallory lowered her voice. "I see now. You're scared. That's what it is! You're scared you'll make it happen. Why did I trust you? What if it was *your* uniform? I didn't see the girl's face."

Meredith stopped and studied her twin's face. "I wasn't scared!" Merry, who was in fact terrified, lied. "Not until now. And worse, you're going to think I didn't do it because I didn't care about another girl getting hurt." *I did care,* Merry thought. *I cared about Kim. Oh, Kim, I should have called you back!* Mally said the girl was little. But any girl would look little on a stretcher! Was Kim going to be hurt?

Or was Kim going to hurt someone?

"I don't really think that," Mallory said softly. "I'm sorry I made fun of you. You're not dumb. But what if it *was* you? It wouldn't be worse, but it would be worse. For me."

"Well, okay. I'll do it. But not because I think you're right. It was . . . how you look now. Weird. And I . . . I would have done something by the end of the day. Was the cheerleader . . . was she hurt . . . hurt?"

"She looked unconscious. She wasn't moving."

"Was it the same thing? Shoe tape?"

"I didn't see anything like that. But she was little. A flyer. So you or Erika or Caitlin. Or Neely. Except I think . . ."

"That Neely's behind it."

"I guess I do but I don't have any reason to think that except she's such a jerk."

"She's not really, Ster. She puts it on. But I don't know why."

"Look," Mallory said. "I'll do it. It's important. I don't want you to change your mind. I actually go past Coach Everson's office now on the way to choir. I'll do it. But what exactly will I say?"

For a moment, Mallory had forgotten that she had a new schedule now. Two weeks before, she'd dropped her second study hall and joined choir. Mallory had no idea why singing suddenly had such a big appeal for her. The tastes she thought she'd have forever were cartwheeling. But she absolutely loved singing the old French traditional songs with their complex unison harmonies and the traditional American gospel and old pop songs. They made her feel the way she felt as a little girl when she first heard "The Moonlight Sonata," happy and tearful at the same time.

Merry thought for a moment. "Just say . . . anything that doesn't sound like me. I can't think. I'll catch up with you between classes because we're already going to be late."

The bell pealed.

"Well," Merry said with a huff, "at least we can take our time now. We both have to go get passes. I'll figure out what to write, and you can drop it off now. Another great benefit of being a medium or whatever we are. So many late passes you get a detention."

The twins were suddenly alone in the hall.

Or so they thought.

"I don't want to interrupt you," Eden said softly. She had appeared beside them without a sound. Like . . . a cat. "I just have a letter for you, Mal. I didn't think you'd want to wait until Friday night for it."

"A letter?" Merry asked. "Who wrote Mallory a letter? Do you have some pen pal?"

"It's a relative of Eden's I met," Mallory said quickly. "It's an athlete."

"It's a guy," Merry said, her smile a bow that unwrapped and widened and widened into a ribbon. "You like a guy."

"Merry!" Mally scolded her. "Don't start now of all times!" The three girls stood in the deserted hallway. Now all three of them needed to go for passes. But the larger question of the envelope in Mallory's hand vibrated in the space between them.

Eden said, "I thought you'd have told your sister."

"Told me what? What? What?" Merry asked, the thought of *Mallory* with a crush blotting all other thoughts from her consciousness. She shifted her huge bag and her books and dropped the purse, and a glittering array of things went flying, from wrist bangles to tubes of lip gloss to spare pairs of shoelaces. All three of them scattered to gather Merry's things, which had rolled under lockers and against closed classroom doors.

"We might as well get Mrs. Dettweiler to include this in the daily announcements tomorrow before the National Anthem," Mally said. "My sister has a mouth bigger than her purse."

"I'm sorry, Mal," Eden said. "I assumed you told her everything."

"Everything?" Mallory exclaimed, widening her eyes significantly.

"I mean, about stuff like this."

"Mallory Arness Brynn," said Merry. "Who is he? Where does he go to school?"

"Boston," Mallory said.

"He's in *college?*"

"No. Prep school."

"Prep school? A preppie? You mean it's . . ."

"Meredith, he's my brother, Cooper. My younger brother. He goes to Boston Flanders."

"I knew it was him! Why didn't you tell me? This is why you walk around the house like a sick cat all the time and don't eat anymore! Cooper! It was at the powwow, right? I'll never ask again if you tell me right now. Even Edie thinks you should tell me."

They'd made their way, walking almost in a moving circle, to the Commons, and the attendance secretary, Mrs. Flecker, was motioning to them from the glassed-in wall of the principal's office.

"Nothing. We walked. And we just talked," Mallory said.

"You made out!"

"No! Not like that!"

"Okay, not like that! But you did something. Dad will throttle you until you are dead."

"But he'll never know because I'll throttle you until you're dead if he does," Mallory said evenly. "Plus, I can't go out with him even if I wanted to."

"He told me that my grandmother gave you an Indian name after all," Eden said.

Mally rolled her eyes, imagining how this sounded to her sister.

Couldn't Edie shut up? By dinnertime, Merry would be telling their parents she was engaged. She pleaded, "Really, Merry, we're just friends."

"But you don't wanna be."

"Maybe," Mallory admitted. "I like him. I like him more than I ever thought I'd like a guy, but he's not here."

"You're wanted in the attendance office," said a familiar voice behind Mallory.

She turned slowly and faced Drew Vaughn.

How long had he been there? Long enough. His normally wisecracker face was rigid as a wooden mask.

Oh, hell, Mally thought. *Now I've hurt my buddy over one kiss that will never mean anything. And why does Drew like me anyhow and what do I care if he does? Except,* she thought, *I do. You can't like two people when you never even considered liking one until a couple of months ago.* Drew turned sharply and walked away. As a RUS (a Responsible Upperclassman Student) he could leave school and roam at will during study halls. He got service credits for helping out in the office. "Drewsky!" Mallory called after him. He didn't look back.

The girls hurried toward the office.

It was the purse dropping and the letter that did it.

For the rest of the day, while Mallory sweated out a test on *The Scarlet Letter* and Merry effortlessly translated *Le Petit Prince,* neither of them thought more about the ambulance dream. They were kids, Mallory would think later, and it was too much.

It was not until Merry was changing into her tryout clothes, mentally practicing her routines and her tumbling, that she remembered that she hadn't left a note for Coach.

They would try out in alphabetical order.

"Brynn" came first.

BASKET CATCH
BASKET CATCH

M eredith had to make a choice. And she had a split second to make it.

Would she hold back and be cautious, for fear that Mally's dream might come true?

Was "might" the key word, she wondered, as she slowly mounted the steps to the stage, measuring mentally how much of a run she could make and still not hit the edge of the stage if she did her round-off, flip, round-off combination? She would have had enough room if she were to do it in her living room (her mother had yelled at her often enough that she would be spending her allowance on lamps for the next year if she didn't stop using Campbell's carpets as practice mats).

She could do it . . . but was a fall the way it was supposed to happen?

Did her own suspicions about Kim cast her old friend in the role of victim or villain?

Ster, she called. She concentrated with all her might. *Ster, tell me. See Kim.* The silence echoed inside her head.

The varsity cheerleaders who would be participating as spotters waited on the stage with big smiles for Merry. She was a favorite. She'd heard the whispers. Little dynamite. The personality-plus twin.

Merry smiled back. But her lip quivered.

Coach Everson said, "Meredith, let's start with the dance to 'Knock 'em Dead.' Okay?"

Merry's heart slowed and her breathing normalized. Nobody could get hurt in a dance. The music began and she concentrated on making her smile natural as she stepped left, left, left, then shook it, shook it, hip, hip, hip—in a circle—then reached, flipped her wrist, dip, high V, drop to one knee.

"Merry, let's try that again with a combination the varsity squad does. Caitlin and Alli, you come up, too. And Neely. Watch Angela and then do it with her," said Coach Everson.

This was no no-brainer dance. Merry had to pay attention. But she didn't miss a step. Next, Kim and the others repeated the same drill. Kim avoided her smile and wouldn't look into Merry's eyes.

But soon, Merry was so into the spirit of the competition that she flipped forward and back with such energy and effort that Pam Door started to applaud before she caught herself.

"You're going to be tough on me," Neely whispered to her.

Because her last name began with a C, Neely came next. Merry couldn't rip her eyes away. Neely was as fluent as rain; she tumbled without a single clump or stammer. From a standing position, Neely could flip front and back—a move Merry still needed her hands to do. It was a display of power that Coach Everson quickly pointed out was unnecessary but impressive. "That's a competition move . . . and not really that either." Coach smiled at Merry, then furiously began making notes.

Neely was blond and had visible boobs and knew how to flirt and was a powerhouse.

"Okay," Coach Everson said, "now stunting." The mounts took the stage and the varsity cheerleaders filled in.

"Merry, let's see a lib and an arabesque and we'll drop into a nice basket catch. Okay now . . ."

They all heard the raucous, deafening metallic alarm. Over and over, it bellowed, the sound a red presence in the air.

Coach Everson stood up. "Girls, follow in an orderly procession. Leave your things here. That's not a planned fire drill."

One after another, the girls walked briskly into the hall, where lines of athletes left practice, all making their way toward the flagpole outside. As the fire engines pulled up and the firefighters plunged into the school, Meredith sidled up to Mallory.

"Did you hear me call you?"

"You mean, was it just luck that the fire alarm went off?" Mally answered without moving her lips. Merry nodded. "No. There's a real fire. In the art room. There's a bunch of papers on fire in a big bin."

"Did you see it? I mean *see* it?" Merry asked.

"I started it. I don't know who pulled the fire alarm," Mallory said. "What else could I do? We forgot all about it because you're so nosy and had to drop your bag!"

Meredith gasped. "You . . . started a fire?"

"Yes."

"And you're blaming me? Because I was shocked that you even had a personal life?"

"Please, let's not end the day with us in jail. Fire isn't dangerous to us. Grandma said."

"It is to other people."

"It was a closed metal bin, Mer, and anyhow, I had to, before the stunting. I just remembered the little gold rings, three rings on two fingers of each hand. I thought of them and I remembered where I saw them. It was at Neely's."

"Neely doesn't have those," Merry said.

"I didn't say she did. I said I saw them at Neely's. Who was your mount?"

"Pam Door and . . . and . . . Kim," Merry whispered.

"Did you look around today?"

"No, I didn't think."

"Well," Mallory said grimly, "I did."

They both glanced at Kim Jellico, who was facing slightly away, watching as the firefighters hauled out the smoking metal bin.

As the timer turned on the school's outside lights in the November dusk, the twins saw six gold rings wink on Kim's small, slender fingers.

TWO FOR THE SHOW

TWO FOR THE SHOW

The morning after the fire that truly wasn't, and the tryout that truly wasn't either, Coach Everson posted a notice on the door of the cheerleaders' changing room: THERE WILL BE NO THIRD SESSION FOR MID-SEASON TRYOUTS. PLEASE MEET AFTER THE LAST BELL IN THE LITTLE THEATER FOR THE RESULTS.

Tingling, Meredith rushed past her classmates and slid into the front row in the little theater, clasping hands with Caitlin.

Coach Everson stepped out onto the stage with Pam Door.

"Girls, there's no reason to attempt a third tryout. We don't seem fated to have one. And in any case, from what we saw, what we have is a dynamite group of junior varsity girls, and you too, Kellen," she added, for the benefit of Crystal's older brother, the only guy on the squad. "But only two of you really stood out as ready for varsity level. It was a very hard choice." Meredith had to gasp: She realized she had forgotten to breathe. "We're going to offer those spots to our old friend Kim Jellico and our new friend Neely Chaplin."

Neely smiled gently and lowered her eyes. "I hope nobody hates me for this," she said softly. Kim got up from her seat and ran from the auditorium.

"NO ONE is going to hate you for it," said Coach Everson. "I'm certain of that. Girls. Girls, am I right? Where's Kim? Well, let's all head into the end of the football season with more spirit than ever before, okay?" There was a stunned murmur of agreement, and several girls turned puzzled, sad faces toward Merry.

No pity, Merry thought.

Though Meredith believed she had turned to stone, she somehow reached out to give Neely's shoulder a squeeze. As Merry gently removed her hand, Neely put her own hand on top of Meredith's.

She whispered, "I can't believe you didn't make it and I did. Especially since you have all the history and you're so cute! I mean, I'm thrilled and I deserved it, but I thought they wouldn't be so open to an outsider!"

You are soooo modest, Merry thought but told Neely, "Coach always says the only fix is talent and hard work. There's no favoritism."

As the rest of the girls, either rushing or pausing to gossip in bewildered knots of two or three, drifted toward the doors, Neely stopped Meredith. "Do you mind if I ask you something? It was like you were, I don't know, distracted. Were you? Am I out of line for asking?"

"No," Merry said. "And yeah, a little. I don't mean you were out of line. I mean, I have a lot on my mind besides cheer squad."

"Do you want to work out with me ever? I mean, I'm not trying to be a jerk. . . ."

In Merry's mind swirled a vortex of images and half-formed thoughts. How bold had her lib stand really been? Had the bobble she felt in her arabesque really been visible? Did Kim move on purpose, to put Merry off balance? Why had Kim been crying in Merry's dream? Who wouldn't be distracted by knowing that her best friend's dead brother would have been a murdering psycho if Merry and Mally hadn't stopped him? David would have killed Merry that day at Crying Woman Ridge, and Kim would never know the hell Mallory went through, hearing Merry cry out for her with her mind, saying good-bye!

But Kim didn't know.

That was the point.

Kim had been out in the dark with some creeps, when she should have been with Merry and her real friends. Kim had nothing to do with David. Kim deserved a little happiness . . . the Kimmie she knew, who made mud cupcakes with her when they were six and the real kind for Will Brent's birthday when they were twelve.

Kimmie.

If she had been out there, alone, getting drunk or worse, was it all Kim's fault? Or was pretty, popular Merry, whose lead everyone followed, just as much to blame?

"So, can you come over again? Maybe Friday?" Neely asked.

"Sure, but right now I have to go see someone."

To Merry's shock, Neely's eyes brimmed. "Yeah. Mallory. I know," she said. "I really always knew you were twins. You have everything. You have a twin and she's cool and she defends you and you have . . . a little sister?"

"A brother. Feel lucky. He's a complete pain."

"But you have one! I don't have anybody or anything but this. Oh, sure, makeup and clothes and CDs and shoes."

Poor baby! Merry thought. *What I wouldn't give up for all that . . . certainly Adam.*

But Neely went on, "Merry, it doesn't make up for your dad being gone half the time and your mom the other half. I mean, I'm absolutely proud of them. But there's not going to be a special dinner tonight at my house because I made it. There would just be a big total silence if I didn't."

Merry's good heart arm-wrestled her writhing envy of the mental picture of Neely with her varsity letter—and won.

"Look," she said. "I'd like to work out with you. And you should hang out with us. Even if we are just small-town girls."

"But I think that's great! Everyone knows everyone else and you're all, like, 'Hi, what did you do last night?' I feel like the princess in the tower."

Oh, please, that has to be so difficult, Merry thought. Neely really had to get a grip on her mouth. But she was probably halfway a decent kid. And *would* Meredith really like to trade the almost-hundred-year-old house on Pilgrim Street for Neely's sprawling brick castle? Yes, she decided, she would—but not Mally, her funny lopsided bedroom or even the thoroughly aggravating Adam. A rush of love for her tough, skinny little brother possessed her. Neely was all alone, and so was Kim. "You put Ridgeline down so much," she said to Neely.

"What do you do if you can't be part of something?"

Pretend like I didn't want it anyway, Merry thought and nodded. She was only half listening to Neely, looking everywhere for Kim. She wanted to hug Kim, and she wanted to sock her. Because of Kim, Merry might not have made varsity. Because of Kim, Crystal had to sit out her season and have months of physical therapy.

But what would drive Kim to do that?

"Maybe I can stay at your house sometime," Neely said shyly.

Huh? Oh, Neely was still there!

Merry said, "Neely, you'd hate it. Nothing is new. Our workout room is a part of the basement that's carpeted. My bathroom is a closet!" But there were advantages to being Neely's friend. *Maybe I can finally try that indoor pool too. Maybe Neely felt warm fuzzies about trading outfits with her really nice but less-fortunate friends.*

"I'd like to come over. Really. Unless you don't want me to."

"Well, sure, but there's no crab puffs and no Bailey's!" Merry said with a laugh. "My mom has antennae and eyes in the back of her head!"

"That's not all bad. She notices you at least," Neely said. "What mother would *let* her kid drink?"

And suddenly, Meredith thought, *I know one who wouldn't.* Bonnie wouldn't, if she could see Kimmie. But Bonnie didn't notice. Not since David died. And how could Kim tell her mom about her lousy friends, that they scared her even as they accepted her, after everything her parents went through already?

Neely got into her big "limo," waving.

Merry zipped up her jacket and shoved her hands into the pockets. It was then that she saw Kim Jellico, in the corner made by the last of the eight school entrance doors and the huge circular wall of the theater. Kim wore her hoodie up and had her face turned into the wind.

"Kim," Merry said softly. Kim didn't look at her. "You made it! I'm so proud of you. You must be so excited." Kim didn't look excited. Merry decided to try an idea. "You know, I just found out the stupidest thing. I'm totally embarrassed because of some of the stuff we say about Coach Everson and guys and stuff in the outfitting room. Did you know there's a video camera in the ceiling in there? I guess they put it in years ago when someone was stealing someone else's stuff out of her locker!"

The face Kim turned to Merry was so pale, her blue eyes so streaked with black mascara tears, that Merry nearly jumped back inside the building.

Softly, Kim said, "There's film of us putting on our uniforms?"

"Out where we put our vests and shoes!"

"That's on film?" Kim repeated, the wind whipping her honey hair, so like David's, in blades across her face. "I think that's illegal."

"No, it's public school," Merry said. "It's a safety issue. Like in the art room, maybe there's one where somebody set that fire."

She was lying, but Kim didn't know that. And everything Kim had done was plain on her face. Merry softened. "Wait, Kim. What if I said that wasn't true? What if I said it just because I suspected someone did something bad to Crystal? And maybe you knew about it."

Kim stared at Meredith. "What do you want me to say?"

"We always told the truth."

"When we were best friends, Meredith. Now who's my friend, Merry? Who wants to be friends with the dead boy's sister? Everyone was so sorry then. Now they treat me like . . . I'm defective. Like I have missing parts."

"You have new friends," Merry said weakly.

"Oh yeah. Real friends. They think any girl's beautiful if her jeans are low enough. And their girlfriends? They're so stoned that . . ."

"No, Kim!" Involuntarily, Merry reached up and covered her mouth, as if by doing that, she could stop Kim from saying anything more, anything worse. But there was no stopping her.

"Do you think my mom doesn't know that Campbell took that job in the ER just because she couldn't stand the sight of my mom suffering? Well, you're right. She doesn't know! She doesn't know anything!" Kim said. "She's like a zombie! But I know. It's like we smell. Remember your mother saying it's just biology? Remember her giving us deodorant? And telling us never to shave our legs above the knees? Remember when she let me sleep over for two weeks, when Mom had her tonsils out? And . . ."

"And how your mom gave us the single pearls on our twelfth birthday and said, now your real life begins? The pearl comes out . . ."

"Of the oyster? And your mom's French toast!" Kim said.

"And my dad's horrible omelets?" Merry put her arms out. "Oh, Kimmie," Merry said. "I'm so sorry. I'm really happy for you about varsity. You didn't mean to do anything wrong. Maybe it'll take away . . ." Kim's face had softened into its former sweetness, but now toughened again. She was so much thinner since David died. Thinner and sharper, hard as an arrowhead.

"Nothing will take anything away. And as for varsity, I don't deserve it! So don't worry about it. Don't even think about it!"

Tim pulled up then. Rolling down the window, he called out, "Do you want a ride, Kim?"

But Kim ran, into the darkness, across the football field toward the thin necklace of lights, more than a mile away, that was Orchard Street, where the Jellicos lived.

Merry called, "Kimmie, wait! It's dark and getting cold!"

But Kim vanished.

Two hours later, as she lay in bed studying, Meredith's telephone made the little waterfall sound that signaled a text message. When she opened it, she saw: I QUIT. HAPPY? KIM J.

NO. CL M! Merry texted back, but her phone was already ringing. And it wasn't Kim.

"Well, hi!" said Coach Everson.

"Hi," Merry replied, terrified that Coach would grill her about the so-called "hidden cameras." But she said something else. "We've had something unexpected happen, Meredith. I'd like you to consider joining varsity. How would you like that?"

"I . . . don't know," Merry said. The dream she had dared to dream came true. Did she even want it? "I know Kim quit."

"This is an honor, Meredith," Coach Everson said, an unmistakable filament of steel springing into her voice.

Merry paused. She said, "Thank you. I'm happy. I'm just sorry for Kim."

"Kim is a very sad young lady right now," said Coach Everson.

A moment later, Neely called. "I heard! We're both on varsity! It's like fate!"

It was just like fate.

In fact, it was fate truly, more than Neely would ever know. But all she could see was Kim's bone-white face. Mallory was subdued, connecting the dots, and even their parents couldn't quite celebrate Meredith's victory, at the expense of Kim's despair.

"I should call Bonnie," Campbell said.

"Would you, Mom?" Merry pleaded.

"You have enough on your plate right now," Tim said. "Later." Campbell sighed.

Mallory had a boy to dream of and Merry literally was on top of the pyramid. They should have been happy. But as they lay in their room, their secrets seemed to circle them like great black birds.

EDEN'S WAY

That Friday evening, Eden and Mallory got into Eden's old truck and headed for the Deptford Mall for the annual pre-holiday sale. Mallory had decided to buy a black skirt, leggings, and a black sweater.

This was unprecedented.

Even Mally couldn't believe she was about to spend hard-earned money on clothes. Other girls did this all the time, but Mallory?

As if she could read her mind—and by now, Mally wouldn't have put that past her—Eden said, "Black's going to make you look like a widow from Sicily. Or with that freckle face, a widow from Ireland."

"But I don't know what colors I like," Mallory said. "I've never bought a skirt and I figured you had to have one black one. I only like maroon and white because it's the Eighty-Niners colors. And red and green because of Christmas!"

"A little limited, Mally! Did you think about whether you're a warm or cool-tone person?"

"Huh?"

"Like, you're a winter color person, but so am I."

"I so have no idea what you're talking about."

"I read it in art. You dress yourself like you would compose a painting. Like, you have gray eyes but they're really dark gray and you have black hair and really fair skin. You don't have pink skin or blue eyes. And I'm a winter person too because I have dark hair and really dark eyes and dark skin. It's an intensity thing. Like, I would look really lousy, semi-dead, in orange and brown. I look good in red and white and black and bright emerald green. Not pastel colors. Rich colors."

"And that's all there is to it?"

"Kind of."

"So . . . say . . . Trevor . . ." Mallory began, referring to the blond forward on their team who had butter-colored hair and eyes—pale, nearly violet.

"She would be a spring. She would wear lemony yellow and pale pink, and it would look good on her and like crap on you. Power colors!"

"Well, let's go for it, then. I've been saving money for two hundred years."

"Then go crazy. Two skirts. Make one, like, purple," Eden suggested.

"You're one to talk," Mallory said.

Eden said cheerfully, "I only get to keep half, for my own

clothes. And my dates don't require a long skirt or even a mini. They require waffle boots and a fleece."

"Yeah, you'd look weird hiding in the brush in a miniskirt."

Eden now spoke openly about James, but in cautious crumbs of information about how they met (she'd been chasing one of her little sisters and literally ran into him) and what he did. What she said made Mallory feel hopeful. In spring, Mallory learned, James left the coppery hills and traveled across the country for his work.

His job was wilderness therapy. He led troubled teenagers on wilderness treks, one or two at a time. If he had girls, he took a girl assistant, sort of an intern. Eden said, "They're not really, like, criminals. That's what James says. Maybe they smoke dope or get lousy grades. But the big thing is their parents don't know what to do with them, so they spend ten thousand dollars to send them to spend six weeks with James. Only a couple of them have been really bad, and he's been doing this for three years. But he's seen a lot of grief for being only twenty-one," Eden said softly. "He started after one year of college. He'll know just what to do and what not to do when he's a father. In a few years, even in a year, the age thing will be like nothing between us. It's just that I'm in high school." Mallory ignored that comment.

"What does he actually do with them? It must be a lot for ten thousand bucks."

"He doesn't get to keep it all! The company gets a bunch of it! And actually, Mal," Eden said, "he mostly listens. Most of these kids are used to being treated like they're in the way. In their own homes. Why do some people have kids? And why do some people who want kids not get to have them?"

Mally decided not to make any comment at this juncture either.

Eden went on, "And sure, he teaches them how to be at home in the wilderness—as if the hills in Cole County are really the wilderness. They're never more than a few miles from a major road. But they have to build their fires and cook their own food and hike for miles, even if it's in a circle, and the stronger ones have to carry food for the weaker ones. They learn they can do more than play with their PlayStations and whine for bigger SUVs."

"He sounds pretty great," Mallory admitted.

"He is," Eden said. "It's not *just* that he looks like the prince in *Sleeping Beauty*. Though that doesn't hurt."

Both girls laughed.

James, Eden went on, never spent more than a few months in each place. Every date with Eden had been an arranged meeting after his fifteen- or sixteen-year-old "students" were bedded down. James was obliged to stay within hearing distance of his students, while giving them independence. But also, Eden confided, making love with a boy, even at her age, would be the same as marrying—breaking her tribal vows.

She wasn't ready to do that before she finished high school. She hoped to get a soccer scholarship and an academic scholarship as well, and to attend a state university close enough so that she could come back and help out when soccer season was over at college.

"But that could change," she told Mallory. "I'm not sure of anything."

Mallory wasn't either. For the first time since fifth grade, she wasn't playing indoor soccer. She had decided to try out for the Cantabiles, the all-girls' concert choir. Miss Yancy had praised her sweet contralto, calling it "a unique voice."

Sometimes, when she looked into the mirror, Mallory didn't know who she was.

"What do *you* get out of it?" Mally asked. "What do you get out of the way you are?"

Eden paused for a long time. She parked her old truck and they hurried through little spits of sleety rain into the Alexis Jones store. The whole first floor looked to Mallory like a display of her sister, except made of white plastic and headless. Dozens of little Merediths-in-shirts-and-vests, Merediths-in-long-tops-and-leggings, Merediths-in-oversize-sweaters sat on top of clear Lucite bins of folded Meredith clothes. Eden pulled out a pleated maroon mini paired with a gray-and-maroon checked shirt. "Try this," she suggested to Mallory.

"It's got those flippy things on the front. I'll look like Meredith."

"You could do a lot worse."

"Thanks!"

"Don't you think Meredith is pretty? Don't you think she has a sense of style?"

"I think she has a wacko obsession with anything even vaguely related to any of her body parts or anything that touches them. She matches her underwear, Edes! Oh, wait, she probably doesn't anymore. Matchy-matchy is out."

"I think matching underwear is nice," Eden said and laughed. "Not that I'll ever have any!" She added softly, "Or that anyone will get to see it." Eden went on, "What do I get out of my thing? Respect. Power. Even adults look up to me. It was fun when I was fifteen. But after I met James . . ."

Dutifully, Mallory tried on the next skirt Eden chose, a mid-calf ballet-type skirt made of light wool. It made Mally feel like a dark flower. She tried to keep her face calm and interested, as if she were really interested in a loose-knit black sweater and striped gray-and-red shirt Eden picked out to go with the skirt. But secretly, her heart was pounding with joy. If James were to leave, before Eden graduated, and Eden had the time to decide to go off to college, maybe their love would end. Her friend would be safe. For now. Lonely, but safe. And James would be safe too, from the bleak aura of menace that surrounded him when his protector, the white puma, crossed his path in Mallory's dreams. Why did Eden take risks when she knew she could hurt James without ever laying a hand—or a paw—on him?

Did he know it would be bad luck for him even to see her?

But Eden would never hurt James, even if he were to see her change.

She would . . . no. Mally wouldn't think about that.

Mally turned to stare at the beautiful tall girl who walked so serenely beside her. Despite everything she knew, it was impossible to imagine Eden's brown eyes contracting into golden orbs, her high cheekbones widening into a broad and sinister parody of her big, white smile. Her skin . . . Mallory's mind rushed away from the image of the lion. James had to be a good person, simply by virtue of the fact that Eden loved him. There had to be more to it, more than the fact that James's love for the Indian girl threatened the prosperity of her extended family. Perhaps James was just a vehicle for Eden, an escape.

With the skirt and sweater and a pair of Mary Janes with one-inch heels in bags knocking against her leg, Mallory and Eden staggered into Pizza Papa.

"I'm weak. I'm violently hungry," Mallory said, pretending to fall into her side of the booth. She looked up and there was Drew, holding out a menu.

"Don't pass out on us, Brynn," he said, with his old Drewsky smile. Mallory was happy to see him happy. Somehow, over the past few weeks, Drew had begun to leave early for school—a clear signal that he wasn't giving the twins a ride as he had for the past two years. But after she and Eden had ordered a large with double cheese and all the vegetables there were, Drew said, "You can ride with me Monday, Brynn. I had to get in early the past few weeks for National Honor Society junk."

"You're in National Honor Society? Drew! Way to go!" Mally jumped up and threw her arms around Drew, as she would have in the old days, but she felt him holding her just a little stiffly, away from him.

"And my girl too!" Drew added.

"Pam is getting inducted? She's a nice girl, Drew, even if she isn't a jock," Mallory said.

"You're dating Pam Door? The cheerleader? Please! You don't like girly girls!" Eden teased him.

Drew shrugged. "Things change. Be boring otherwise. I'll get your 'za."

Eden whispered, "I always thought he had a crush on you!"

Mallory said, "Things . . . change."

"What did Cooper say in his letter?" Eden asked. Mallory almost didn't answer. She was lost in a memory of Drew's Green Beast, the hideous Toyota truck, coming like a chariot to save her and Merry when David cornered them in the deserted construction site. She thought of Drew's strong arms around her, patting her head, telling her it was okay. Drew . . . the only person outside the little circle she trusted. What she felt for Cooper wasn't trust, it was attraction. It wasn't old, but new and exciting. And still, that wasn't the same as tested and true. She was totally happy that he was with Pam. Except she wasn't. If Cooper was a comet, Drew was the North Star, always the same, always steady, looking down on her.

Mallory noticed Eden waiting. She said, "Well, he told me that your grandma gave me the name Wapiw, although I don't know if I'm saying it right."

"It means 'to see.' And I don't either because it's been so long since there were native Cree speakers that even people in the same clan kind of have their own way of saying things."

"So she knows about me."

Eden said slowly, "Grandmere's not like . . . you. But she can tell some things. She's lived a long time. She's eighty-five."

"Get out! She looks so young!"

"My mother is forty-eight, and she has a three-year-old. In my family, the women have lots of babies and late."

"Wow. My mother would fall over and die from exhaustion if she had a baby now."

"Most people don't have eight kids, for sure."

When the pizza arrived, Mally couldn't help being distracted by Drew working behind the counter, cleaning up. When they were little kids, Drew's red hair and big teeth made him look like a cartoon or a puppet. But now, his hair was styled long on top and cut short over the sides and had darkened to a deep, velvety auburn. Years of cross-country had given him strong legs and broad, flat muscles across his shoulders and chest. Braces had restructured his smile. Drew, Mally realized, was . . . more than just nice.

"What else did Coop say?"

"Just that, really, and he gave me an address where I could write to him. They don't let them have e-mail."

"Well, he's coming home in two weeks for a month! I'm so happy. I want him to meet James. He'll see then. He will, Mally."

Cooper, home for a month. Why hadn't he told her? And what could they do? The fact remained that Mallory, despite having lived a lifetime since last winter, wouldn't be fourteen for another month and a half and wasn't allowed to date until she was fifteen.

"You'll come out and see him," Eden said then, as if reading Mallory's thoughts.

"I have to go back to the department store," Mally said.

"Did you forget something?"

"Pants. Power colors. Intense, winter-white shirts. I've had six pairs of the same kind of jeans since I was in seventh grade. I just had my mom order more of them after they wore out."

"You're going downtown, Mally!"

"You bet," Mallory said.

But even as she laughed and pretended to be a girl-on-a-spree, she was thinking that Cooper would no more want to meet James than she would want to meet David Jellico's twin.

Gesturing with her pizza crust, gossiping about how much Eva Wiley's shoes cost and how many pairs Eva had, using her index fingers to stroke her long hair in ribbons behind her ears, laughing until she snorted her soda, Eden looked like any other beautiful girl.

But she wasn't.

Mallory wished she could talk about all this to Meredith! But Merry was deep in some lost place these days. She came home early and exhausted from the new demands of varsity cheerleading and stayed quiet, moody. And so Mallory kept Eden's confidence locked away, just as she kept Cooper's kiss. Two things that meant everything to her—they might never mean a thing to the world outside the private tower room that had become her heart.

THE HUNTER

THE HUNTER

On a Friday night the week before Thanksgiving, Tim picked
the twins up from choir and cheer practice and swung past
the hospital to get Campbell. Worn out from an after-school
snowball fight and the beginning of his own indoor soccer season,
Adam was asleep in the back, slumped sideways in his seat belt.

Tim left the car idling in the circle but he immediately came
rushing back out.

"Girls, we might have to leave without her," he said, pulling the
van off to one side as not one but two ambulances, the Boone and
Cole County fire department vehicles, swung into the bay.

Frozen, fascinated despite the ugliness of the lights against the
dark-denim mackerel sky, the twins and Adam watched as the
medics threw open the doors and ejected two men roughly bound
to stretchers. Both of them wore vests of hunter orange with tufts of
stuffing like cotton candy at the places the paramedics had cut away

buttons and sleeves. Bags of the liquid Mally and Merry knew was called Ringer's were attached to their hands by needles. Campbell rushed out, another nurse behind her.

"Okay, what have we got here?" she asked. She seemed to see her children but not to look at them.

"Thigh laceration, thirty centimeters or more, no involvement with the femoral artery but some kind of fracture...and considerable blood loss," said the paramedic, a woman from Ridgeline who had a kid in Adam's grade. Mally climbed out of the backseat to watch.

"Get a type and match stat and X-ray," Campbell said. "Dr. Pennington is on. Not the father, the young woman. The resident. Which is lucky. She's an orthopedic surgeon. What about the kid?"

There was a kid?

"He's fourteen, fifteen. We don't know what the heck is wrong with him. He's shocked, though. He says his uncle was attacked by a lion he shot at," said the medic from the Cole County Fire and Ambulance. "They were looking for deer up on the ridge."

Campbell quickly repeated everything to the doctor who ran beside her as they rushed the victims through the huge swinging doors. Mallory recognized Dr. Pennington as the woman who'd looked at her head.

"She's something else," Merry finally said. "Mom, I mean, not the doctor."

"Yep. She knows her stuff," said Tim, admiration suffusing his voice.

"Why doesn't she become a doctor?" Mally asked.

"I think someday she might."

The twins and Adam simultaneously squawked, "What?"

"We think," Tim said, "Mom may go to medical school."

"She's forty-three years old, *DAD*!"

"And that would mean what?" Tim asked. "She's already got a master's in nursing, which cuts way down on her time, and she'll be a resident in at the most four years. She'll practice for twenty years or more."

"Is this what all this stuff is about?" Merry asked.

"All what stuff?" Tim asked.

"All this stuff about Mom being tired and junk."

"Actually, no, that's not what it's about," he said.

"Because this has been going on for months," Mally said. "She's exhausted. She's cranky. She's moody."

Tim said, "She's pregnant."

"She's *what?*" Merry nearly screamed.

"She's pregnant," Tim said again, dropping his voice. "And if you tell her I said—"

"She's pregnant with a baby?" Adam asked.

"That's . . . how it usually goes," Tim said.

"Dad, don't goof around. MOM is pregnant?" Mally persisted.

"Look! Do you think we found you under Grandma's rosebushes?" Tim was finally exasperated. "She'll kill me so please, please act surprised when she says something about . . ."

"Mom is going to have a baby and study to be a doctor?" Mally went on. "Take my temperature, Meredith. I'm feverish."

"Not at the same time," Tim said. "She'll take some time off and then Aunt Karin . . ."

"Aunt Karin's having another baby?"

"No," Tim said of his sister. "Aunt Karin will take care of the baby while Mom works part-time and goes to school part-time. Sheesh! That's part of the master plan. She took the job in the ER before this happened."

"Happened?" Merry asked. "It happened, like a thunderstorm?"

"We didn't plan it," Tim said. "Gosh, this is pretty personal."

"It's just biology!" Merry and Mally teased him, again simultaneously.

"These things happen," Tim said.

"And you're always on our case about, 'When you're thirty-five, you have to use two kinds of birth control.'"

A woman and a young teenager, people Mally assumed were family to the hunter and the kid, rushed past them, their tearful faces maps of strain and worry. For a moment, the Brynns were silenced by their grief.

Then Tim went on fending off his daughters' assault. "By the time you're thirty-five, you'll be married," he said. Tim began to walk toward the doors of the emergency room.

"What about us?" Adam yelled.

"We're planning on keeping you," Tim said casually, shoving his hands into his jacket pockets. But the three kids leaped out of the car to chase him.

"I thought Adam was the accident," Meredith went on.

"Perfection is never an accident," Adam replied, pulling up the sleeve of his fleece to display his minute bicep.

"Really, Dad," Meredith went on. "Mom said she didn't

necessarily plan to have Adam . . . that you guys just didn't try to stop him. Aren't you a little old for this?"

"Movie stars do it all the time," Tim said, taking a seat in the ER lobby and seriously studying a copy of *Sports Illustrated* that was at least two months old.

"The Cubs won the Series, Dad, which means they got into the play-offs," Mallory told him, peering at him over the top of the magazine. "It happened two months ago, which means you aren't reading that magazine. You're avoiding us. What you're saying is that you were irresponsible. And now Mom is going to possibly die from having a baby too late in life!"

"Mallory Arness Brynn, sit down," Tim finally said. "You're smart, and you certainly have the most opinions per pound in the family. But this is none of your business. Your mother has wanted another child for years. I didn't when the business was getting up and running. And she figured she'd never do it once she was in medical school. So we gave it a short period of trying and . . . it worked. And by the way, she's fine. And so is your little brother."

"A boy? A guy baby?" Adam pumped the air with his fist.

"Our little brother? You can already tell?" Merry marveled.

"Mom is more than four months along in her pregnancy," their father said, as though he were reading the news.

Adam began counting on his fingers.

"He'll be born around my birthday!" Adam said. "We could name him Alphonse or Amadeus or . . ."

"Artichoke, or maybe Math Genius!" Mallory said. "It took you five minutes to think of how many months there were between four and nine! Ant, be quiet. This means . . . they were fooling around again when we were up on vacation at the camp." Once again, eleven years after Adam's birth, Tim and Campbell evidently forgot all the lessons they had played with all the subtlety of the percussion section of a marching band, during their two-week vacation up at the Brynn family's cabins.

Mallory almost forgave them. The camp was the place where they all forgot their real selves and simply played, kids and grownups alike. Even though they were almost grown, at least in their own eyes, and even though their "vacation" took place no more than ten miles from their front step, the twins still loved the cabin camp, and their time there with their cousins—fishing and swimming in the Tipiskaw River that rumbled over the rocks below Crying Woman Ridge. Nobody thought about makeup or gossip or homework. Days began slowly and ended even more so.

While Campbell sometimes grumbled that other families went to Disney World, when they had gone there, the year Adam was six, the girls actually preferred throwing potatoes into the fire pit to cook to riding the latest roller coaster at Epcot.

Some of their father's great-uncles and their families still came to the camp during the two full summer months that Grandma and Grandpa spent up there, from July until school. Mallory never entirely understood that, because Grandma Gwenny had more gardens than an English countess and had to pay a kid to weed them while they were "gone," though they probably could have seen their yard from the top of the ridge. Mallory knew that the roses, for example, were at their most glorious when Gwenny wasn't there, though she drove down a couple of times a week to bring huge cuttings up to the camp and to the nursing home.

"I'm old," Grandma Gwenny said. "I can have it both ways. I'm going to come up to this camp as long as I can walk."

The first two weeks of July were reserved for Tim's family and his brothers and sisters. Everyone was there to watch the ring of fireworks displays from all the towns around Ridgeline, from Deptford to Kitticoe all the way out to Warfield, nearly twenty miles away.

It was, Campbell once said happily, like having a ringside seat for summer.

Later in the year, often after Christmas, they visited Campbell's father in Virginia for a week. He visited them, in turn, at Easter time.

But evidently, it was always and only the camp that made their parents get all peppy. Mally wasn't quite sure how to feel about the baby. Of course, he would be adorable. He would be so adorable that leaving him to go to college when he was only three would probably break her heart. On the other hand, it would probably keep Campbell and Tim from going mental with loneliness once all of them were gone.

But what if he had terrible birth defects because Campbell was so old? Mallory knew that tests revealed most of those things, but tests weren't infallible! Campbell could practically be a grandmother!

Tim looked up. "Why are you pouting?" he asked. "We're both very happy about the baby. Now, if that emergency is under control . . ."

"I don't want to change any diapers," Adam said firmly.

"Girls think it's sexy," Merry told him.

"Hence my decision," Adam replied.

"What decision?" Campbell asked. All of them nearly levitated out of their chairs. And no one said a word. Behind them, they could still hear the man screaming about a "critter."

"What's he talking about?" Tim asked.

"What are you talking about?" his wife asked in return, pushing the sleeves up on her sweater, as if prepared to do combat. "As if I didn't know plain as the nose on my face, Tim Brynn."

"Medical school," Adam said virtuously. "I think it's very brave of you to try to learn things at your age, Mom."

"Campbell, really, what is he on about?" Tim asked.

"He says he was attacked by a mountain lion. He smells like he fell into a distillery. I suppose it's possible he could have encountered a bear way up there. He was deer hunting. Said he got a shot off that sliced its leg but it ran away. You don't think an old guy from Mount Kisco is smoking dope, do you?"

"No, but it's weird," Tim pointed out, grateful that Campbell wasn't pushing his discussion with the kids. "Is the boy okay?"

"He is," Campbell said. "But he swears he heard it growl too. I think he turned to run and hit his head or something. He's got a bump but he'll be fine. Why people take twelve-year-olds hunting is beyond my comprehension." She shrugged into her coat and went on, "It is weird enough that they're going to bring an animal control officer all the way from Warfield tomorrow morning. If there's any kind of predator up there, behind Rose Reservoir, she'll track it with dogs. It'd probably have to have been some kind of coyote. But it's strange that the Polk kid said the same thing."

Madly, Mally was texting Eden into her phone. CM. 2BAD2BT. When no familiar text floated on down with a waterfall of electronic tones, she punched in Eden's number.

"It's Eden! Leave a message and hope for the best!" said the familiar voice, with its nearly imperceptible lilt.

"No, Eden! No! Damn!" Mally whispered. As if Eden could answer her anyhow . . . from up on Rose Ridge.

Mallory shoved her phone back into her pocket. She was going to have to find a way, to get out past the Rose Ridge reservoir herself, which was about as far from her house as she'd ever run, more than ten miles. Her parents warned her not to go up there with anyone, because of the reservoir's reputation. Boy Scouts dutifully picked up beer cans there every spring,   but there would always be a whole new crop by fall. Down in the water, the rear end of at least one old car stuck up like something out of a horror comic.

How would she find someone who could help? And if she found Eden, who would she be?

By now, Cooper was home, but there was no way she was going to be able to get all the way out to the Cardinal tree farm tonight. She didn't know if he even had a cell phone. Eden's uncles were there working with her father for the Christmas tree season, with several of her boy cousins. She'd told Mallory that this year Grandmere had made dozens of pairs of tiny baby moccasins ordered by people all over New England. In the bottom of each tiny gathered bit of foot-shaped hide, Annaisa poked a hole. Lots of people put them on their Christmas trees for babies born that year, Eden explained. The moccasins weren't for wearing. By poking the tiny hole, her grandmother said, she gave the parents a powerful symbol, the wish that the baby would live long enough to wear out a thousand pairs of moccasins. It all sounded so ordinary and Eden-like and normal.

Mallory couldn't wait to see Cooper. She'd even been practicing putting her hair up in different ways—something she was as likely to do as to dye it purple. When she thought of him, her stomach still whirled. She'd lost five pounds since Halloween, something her mother noticed and criticized. Now, all she felt when she thought about Cooper was anxiety.

Of course, she could be completely wrong.

Maybe the older guy did run into a bear. It happened out there every couple of years to deer hunters. Maybe he cut himself on a branch and was too drunk to confess.

For why would Eden do such a thing?

Why?

Mallory didn't know why. All she knew was that she had to know.

AT THE VERGE

AT THE VERGE

P lease, Drewsky, please, please," Mallory begged.

"No, Brynn, no, no," Drew Vaughn answered.

"Why?" Mallory exploded into the phone. "I would for you."

"You always say that. And yet, you have never driven me anywhere or done anything remotely weird or life-risking for me because, hey, you can't! You're not even fourteen."

"But I would if I could and you know it! An hour at most, Drew."

"Not an hour at most because it'll take an hour just to get there and back on a Friday night, and then you have to do whatever nuts thing you have to do."

"Okay, an hour and a half at most. You'll be home by eight-thirty. The glitter people never go out before ten."

"Well, my parents glitter me home at one at the latest, not that you should tell anyone that. Or else the Green Beast turns back into a pumpkin. I'm dating a senior. Give me a break."

"Drew, I wouldn't ask you if I could ask anyone else," Mallory wheedled.

"That's nice of you. Good old Drew, the last choice."

"I didn't mean it that way and you know it. You're the only one I can ask, for obvious reasons."

"Well, it's still no, and for obvious reasons. First of all, it's dark and I don't have this big desire to go driving up the crummy road by Rose Ridge reservoir when the dopers have probably been there since three-thirty this afternoon. Second, I have a date. And third, I have a date."

"Okay, fine," Mallory said, her voice flat.

"What do you mean, okay fine?"

"Okay fine. Don't take me. And don't ever, ever, ever ask me for another favor again as long as we live. Don't ask me to do your trig on the way to school. Ever. Don't ask if you can use my iPod. Don't ask me to run with you so you can time yourself."

"Brynn, what the hell?" Drew was honestly bewildered. "What could you want in the dark out there that can't wait until morning?"

"I said forget it."

"Good grief! I'll pick you up in fifteen minutes," Drew said. "If it's something nuts, I swear I'll never give you a ride to school again. You can ride the bus like the teeny little freshman nothing that you are."

"Oh, Drew, thank you! Thanks so much! I totally love you for this!"

But Drew had already hung up the phone. Mally ran to pull on her windbreaker over her Spandex running pants and tied a scarf around her neck. She rummaged around until she found Adam's stocking cap and the miner's headlamp he'd taken to his sixth-grade sleepover camp.

She had no idea how far up she'd have to walk. She and Drew had driven up to the top of the hill above the reservoir with the intention of going swimming one day just after he got his driver's license, but there was a loud party going on that repelled them right away. Girls were swimming in their underpants and bras. Even if Drew would have liked looking, he didn't want Mallory there and said so. But it was probably no more than a mile, and maybe less. If there was anything to see, she knew she'd see it . . . or hear it. If there were hunters, they would be back down at the Camelot or the Holiday Inn. An hour and a half, she had promised Drew—while promising her parents that she had to help Drew pick out flowers for Pam's birthday (Mallory had no idea when Pam's birthday actually was). What she was worried about was encountering some high-school stoners sitting in the scrubby trees up there and wondering if she would dare to explain to them why they should go home or if they'd fall into the reservoir laughing.

Even so, there was no alternative but to try.

"I know what you're up to," Meredith said, as she put the finishing touches on her outfit, her melon skirt from last year's birthday party paired with blue leggings and a new blue sweater. She was going to Neely's and was cheerful for the first time in ages. Mally spun around to face her sister, stark panic on her face. "It's about that guy. Cooper. Eden's brother. You're sneaking out to meet him."

Arranging her panicky glare into an eager girl-crush face, Mallory made Merry promise. "Don't tell." Grinning, Merry took time from her dressing ritual, which Mallory had clocked at ninety minutes, to use two fingers to cross her heart. And then Mallory was out the door.

Assuming from her headlamp and clothing that she was going running after picking flowers, Campbell shouted for Mally to be quick about it, but Mally called back that she might drop in and see Eden, who might be waitressing at the Big Dipper. Campbell was drowsy. Tim and Adam were playing chess.

And so Mallory slipped out under the cover of everyone else's preoccupation.

THE CAT

THE CAT

Mallory's resolve shuddered.

It was smudge-smoke dark on the road that led up and around Rose Ridge reservoir. Six or seven junky cars—junkier even than Drew's—were parked in the scrubby trees at the side of the road. She could hear hoots and shouts down by the water, even though it was cold enough outside to see her breath.

Although he promised to stay in the car, Drew made Mallory agree to use a signal—three short flashes of the light and one long one—if she got in trouble and needed him, which he warned her she had better not. Drew was dressed for his date, wearing a pair of cuffed chinos and a pale green sweater. When Mallory told him he looked nice, Drew ignored her.

She used her headlight to keep to the path, such as it was, as she scuffled her way uphill. Every few moments, she would call out in a soft voice, "Eden! It's Mallory!" But nothing stirred. The partiers' distant noise faded. The wind rattled the dry branches and something small and quick slithered across the trail behind her. She heard the occasional loud crash from below and saw flames leap as someone threw something on the bonfire.

Mallory walked faster, her hands deep in her pockets.

She made her way up to the top of the ridge over the reservoir and peeked down at the party. Mostly guys with a few girls wearing shorts or sweats, they were yelling and singing and throwing green beer bottles into the now-raging fire. Every time one crashed, Mally jumped.

She smelled the lion behind her before she saw her.

It was a strong, wild, hot scent like nothing Mallory had ever experienced, cleaner than a zoo smell, not unpleasant but tangy and strong. She heard the low sound that ended in the "wow" of a snarl.

Slowly, she turned, steeling her body to remain still. Was this really Eden? If it was, could Eden's mind be inside the creature?

Determined not to flinch, Mallory couldn't help but fall back a step when she actually saw the lion. It was not really white but a buff color, like brushed suede boots or sheepskin. It would have been magnificent had Mally not been so terrified. No more than ten feet away, it stood among the low birches, its unblinking golden eyes with their straight-line black pupils fixed on her, the muscles of its chest and forelegs like tiny mountain ranges. Its head was twice the size of Eden's, its grin between thin black lips one of the most frightening things Mallory had ever seen. It . . . no, she . . . tossed her head and snarled again. An electrical thrill pulsed along Mally's arms.

Mally took a deep breath.

"Eden?" she said.

The cat delicately placed one paw before the other and stepped toward Mallory. Mallory's bladder tightened. She nearly turned to run; instead, she squeezed her eyes closed and prayed to St. Bridget. She smelled and felt, rather than saw, the big cat's approach, shivered as its casual heft brushed her leg—the cat's shoulder higher than Mallory's hip.

Mallory breathed then.

It could have killed her.

So it was Eden.

"You hurt that man. Eden, why? Is that the kind of bad luck Cooper meant? How can that be good? Hide, Edie. Please. An animal control officer with a big rifle is coming tomorrow from Warfield. Do you hear me? Do you understand me?" Mallory looked deep into the golden eyes and heard Eden tell her, the way Meredith did, *I do.*

Then she heard the voice.

"You don't belong around here, little dude." The voice was twangy with menace. Mally turned, her hood slipping back. There were two of them—one guy small and scrawny with a caterpillar 'stache and the other bulky with eyes as blank as a bear's. "Oh, the dude's a lady. Ry, look here. A mini-lady has come to visit us. Hi, baby."

Eden was . . . where? Nowhere to be seen.

"I . . . I was running," Mallory said. "I'm just going down."

"That's okay," said the skinny boy, who had buzz-cut black hair to go with his mini-mustache. "You come on down by us and have a brew."

"No thanks."

"No, you come on down. Right, Ry?"

"No. I'm only twelve."

"You're pretty cute, though. I was brewing up a storm when I was twelve. No time like the present to get started." The skinny boy with the black buzz stepped forward and grabbed Mallory's arm.

"Leave me alone!" she said sharply. "My brother's down there."

"Let him come too, then. We don't want you going to tell Mommy what you saw at the reservoir, right?"

Pulling her miner's light off her head, Mally switched it on-off three times and then back on. "Ooooooooh," said Buzz Head. "Secret code."

"I know her," said the other boy, the one called Ryan. "That's the little chick that was on TV when that big fire happened. The twin. And she was the one there when the guy went over the cliff in Ridgeline. That was intense. Did his head break like a pumpkin? Was it sick?"

"Leave her alone, you idiot," said a familiar voice. Kim stepped out from behind the Buzz Head boy. "Mally, is that you?" Mallory nodded. Kim wore a sweatshirt ripped open to the top of her bra, and a parka. Her skintight black jeans were stuffed into furred boots that outlined her calves. "Evan, she's a little kid. She's my friend's sister. Let her alone."

"I'm no more a kid than you, Kim. Why are you here?"

"Why do you care?" Kim asked. Whipping a lighter out of her

parka pocket, she stumbled a little. In the light from her headlamp, Mally saw that Kim's eyes were black pits at the center, wavering and bloodshot. The cigarette was just a Marlboro, but there was more going on than that. Mallory didn't know whether to be more afraid of Kim or the boys. More were making their way up the hill.

"Ev!" one called. "Evan! What are you doing, Tauber? Taubsky? What's going on? Where's Kim?" A guy at least a head taller than Drew stepped out onto the path. His head was shaved and, in the cold, he wore nothing but a T-shirt with the sleeves ripped off and "Dead Meat" scrawled on it in crude strokes of marker. "Who's the midget?"

"Leave her alone, Evan, Brett. She's leaving. She was just up here for a run," Kim said.

"Kim, come home with me. Drew's down there. We'll drive you."

"My parents would just love to smell my breath now," Kim said, with a laugh that came out more like a croak. The bare-headed boy, Evan, grabbed her arm and kissed her deeply. Kim broke away. "You go home, Mally." She dragged deeply on the cigarette. "My friends are nicer to me than the stuck-up little preps and princesses at Ridgie."

"I'm sure they're nice, but Kim, you're not even fifteen."

"Since when?" the boy asked.

"She's nuts," Kim said. "I told you. I'm a senior."

Mallory said, "She's not. She's a freshman. Just like me. Her brother was the boy who died in Ridgeline last spring. The one who fell off the cliff. Deirdre's guy. You just said. *She's* just a kid. You're giving beer and cigarettes to a *kid*. And I'm going to say so. I recognize you. And I don't care what you think. I heard your name. Evan Tauber. I'll tell the cops."

"I don't think you will," the bald-headed giant said gruffly. "I don't think you'll want to tell anyone if you hear what might happen to you if you open your mouth, little teeny girl." He grabbed one of Mallory's arms, but Kim reached for Mally's other hand. The boy called Ryan pushed Kim's hand away, nearly knocking her down. Mallory struggled, as the bald giant held her tighter.

Then they all heard the high, impossibly loud cry, humanlike but not human.

Behind them, the mountain lion crouched on a rock.

She rolled her shoulders and growled again, her claws like individual teeth, her teeth glistening in a mouth that yawned so large Mally could have put her head and shoulders inside it. The cat lay low on the boulder, her head restlessly swinging. The moon had risen, bathing the path in white light. The puma looked cut from marble, like a statue of a beast, except that it moved.

"Mother . . . man, what is that?" Ryan whispered, backing up.

"You're lit, man," said the skinny guy

"You see it too."

"I think I'm seeing what I smoked. I'm out of here. . . ."

"It can't be there, because it can't exist. Even though we're seeing it. It can't be," said Buzz Cut. Their friend had already cut out for the scrubby path downhill.

"What is?" Kim asked. "What's that sound?"

The huge guy was looking over Kim's head at the cat and beginning to back down the slope.

"It's really there," Mallory said to the guys. To Kim, she said, "Kimmie, listen. For your mom's sake. For David's sake. Listen. Look right at me and walk down the path. I'm so serious, Kim. Don't turn around."

As if hypnotized, Kim began to walk down the ridge path toward the parking lot. The cat snarled again. Kim began to run. Mally followed her.

"I'm gone. Tell Jaybird and Detox to grab a ride." The boy called Ryan began to jog down the path. Buzz-cut was nowhere to be seen. The huge bald guy had just turned his back when Eden sprang. She sailed ten, maybe fifteen feet, like something light instead of something that weighed easily four times what Mally did, but she hit the ground in long, easy running leaps and was almost upon the giant within seconds.

"Eden, no!" Mallory shrieked. "He didn't hurt me!"

Kim had disappeared.

Mallory heard the shrieks and scrambling from below as everyone made for their cars. As Mallory watched, Eden closed the distance between her and the scrawny boy with the ripped T-shirt; she saw his face as he glanced back once, bone-white with fear.

And then Eden fell.

She fell flat just a foot from where she had caught up to the boy, taking a first step and then stumbling into a copse of low bushes.

"NO!" Mallory cried. "NO!"

She hadn't heard a shot. The animal control wasn't supposed to come until tomorrow.

She turned the light toward where Eden lay and ran to her side. Kneeling, she ran her hands over the tiny spot of blood on the cat's thigh. She heard a stick break behind her and looked up into Cooper's face, his wonderful face she'd missed so much. Mally cried, "What did you do to your sister? How could you hurt her?"

"It's okay," Cooper said, pulling her close to him, kissing her hair, then her mouth. She could see that he was crying. "There were herbs on the arrow. From our grandmother. She'll sleep an hour and then head north. I heard on the radio that she hurt that man. That's the ancient way. I don't think she meant to hurt him." Cooper held Mallory close to him and said, "I'm scared to death. What if I hadn't hit her? And it's Eden! How could I do this to Eden? I never thought it would be like this."

Mallory pulled away.

"How did you think it would be? Did you think Eden would just be happy being everyone else's fairy godmother? Is this okay with you? That your sister takes out the occasional little old man who has the bad luck to see her, just because it's the *ancient way?*"

"No, but Edensau should stay away from people!"

"Maybe she's mad, Cooper. Maybe she's lonely! She's taking too many chances."

"But that old man told what he saw," Cooper went on. "And those stoner kids are going to tell too."

"No they won't. They'd have to explain what they were doing down there. Everybody knows what Rose Ridge means."

"True. But she has to hide. The animal control . . ."

"I know, Cooper. The old man shot at her! He said he did, at the hospital. My mom was there. She treated the guy and his grandson.

He shot at her with a gun. If he wasn't so drunk he'd have hit her."

"He did hit her," Cooper said, leaning over Eden's fallen form. Mallory clutched his arm. "But, look, she's okay. The bullet barely creased her skin. Right there. That hide is tough."

"But Eden's hide isn't! Will it show on her real skin?"

"I don't know. Why do you keep blaming me? I love her as much as you do! She's been scratched by branches, yes, and growled at by bears. But never hurt. She's tough. She's stayed out of sight and safe. I don't know what's come over her!" Cooper raked his hair back with both hands.

"James has."

Cooper let his breath out in a rush. "Of course. That's why."

"Is something going to happen to us? Because we saw her?"

"I don't think so," said Cooper. "I'm under her protection. I assume you are too. And anyway, I'm not having particularly good luck tonight."

"And my luck is generally bad."

Cooper said, "This is a hell of a mess, Mallory." In his dark shirt and jeans, he looked like part of the sky, part of the dark trees and suddenly starless sky. Star blanket. His name. Mallory couldn't have seen Cooper if he hadn't been standing so close. Suddenly, he took her hand. "I think about you all the time. Why do you have to be such a kid?" He kissed her again. Mallory, ready this time, leaned into him and kissed him too, reaching up to put her arms around his neck. Cooper pulled her close to him. She felt the buckle of his belt against her sternum. There would be a mark there.

She was glad.

"So, okay, this is why I had to drive you up here?" Drew Vaughn asked coldly. "So you could meet him?"

Burrs clung to the cuffs of Drew's good pants, and he reached up to pull a branch from his hair. "I saw your light, Brynn. I thought you were in trouble."

"I was. Those boys down there . . ."

"Right. Was he with them?"

"You know he wasn't. This is Eden's brother."

"I know who it is," Drew said. "I get it now. Thanks a lot, Brynn. Remind me to help you out again sometime real soon."

Pulling away from Cooper, Mallory raised both hands in a gesture almost like a prayer. "Please don't think that, Drew. I would never use you like . . ."

"Your mom and dad would go nuts if they knew you were going out to meet him, but it's okay if good old Drewsky is there. They can trust me! What do you think that's like?" Drew spat the words on the ground. "Hey, Cooper. You take her home. And don't worry about Kim. Some psycho in a Buick picked her up. I think she broke one of her high heels, though."

He turned his back and jogged away down the hill.

Mally turned back to Cooper. He was using a bough to sweep away the tracks and kicking around stones to remove the signs of a scuffle. He kneeled again next to Eden, placing his hand on the thick pelt, where a ruff of white bunched at the neck. "She's breathing easily."

"I'm not!" said Mallory. "Eden is my best friend! Drew Vaughn has known me all my life."

"And he likes you, not just like a friend, and he saw us over there. What can I do about that? I like you not just like a friend too."

"But he thinks I'm a loser and a user," Mally said as Cooper picked up his bow. "I only wanted to warn Eden."

"That's the price you pay," Cooper said.

"Easy for you to say if you don't have to pay it."

"I do," Cooper said. "That's my sister! This is my big sister on the ground. I shot her with the bow she helped me make when I was twelve and she was fourteen. How do you think I feel? How would you feel?"

"Horrible. I'm sorry. I'm so sorry. I know."

"Do you have to go right home?" Cooper asked suddenly.

"I'm cold and dirty. And yeah."

"Right home, right this minute?"

"Why?"

"This night is a nightmare. Only one good thing can come out of it so . . . I thought we'd sit for a moment and look at the stars. The truck is down there."

"It's cloudy now. There are no stars to see."

"Oh, well," Cooper said, and smiled—a smile weary but real.

"I'm almost fourteen."

"I just turned sixteen. Two years and a couple of weeks between us. My grandmother was fourteen when she married my grandfather," said Cooper. "But you don't have to worry about anything, Mallory. I like you, but I would never hurt you or make anything difficult for you that way."

"I know that," Mally said. She took his hand.

"And I'll get you home in a while. Honest Injun."

"Don't say stuff like that."

"I'm just goofing."

Cooper was as good as his word, but for the first time in her life, Mallory went home with "kissing chin." No one but Merry noticed because it was almost gone by morning—except for the memory, both tart and sweet.

LITTLE BROTHER

LITTLE BROTHER

Within a few weeks, Campbell's pregnancy was obvious. And still, nobody had said anything definite about where a nursery would be—or anything else. It was becoming absurd, Meredith thought. Their mom had begun leaving the top buttons open on her jeans a few weeks before and was wearing Tim's worn-out dress shirts at home. *If it's up to her,* Merry thought, *she'll tell us when she's on the way to the hospital!*

On the first morning of Christmas break, Coach was sick and there was no practice. Merry sat down beside Campbell in the kitchen. Campbell glanced up over the tops of her rimless reading glasses and smiled.

"Why are you staring?" she asked.

"Can you feel it yet?" Merry asked.

"I can, but you won't be able to for another month or more," Campbell said. "So why didn't you just say something if you knew? All you do is stare."

Unnoticed, Mallory slipped into the kitchen and began lacing up her running shoes. She hadn't done her run in a few days, couldn't sleep or eat, and thought she might be losing her mind. She barely noticed her mother and sister.

"I'm staring at you because I want to say something and I don't want you to kill me," said Meredith.

"Merry Heart, other than telling me that you're pregnant too, there's not much you could say that would make me go savage when I'm sitting here eating cinnamon toast."

"So it's okay to mention that you're . . . you know, pregnant."

"Yes, it's okay. I am . . . you know, pregnant. And when we have a baby, we won't have to keep him inside so that people won't realize he's around." Campbell put down the book she'd been reading. "I know I'm old to have a baby. That's why I've been uncomfortable talking about it. I was very afraid I'd lose the baby. It's stupid, but it seemed easier not to talk about it if there was that risk."

"Mom," Merry said then. "The problem is, I don't think you thought this through. When this baby is thirty, you'll be seventy-three."

"Geez," said Campbell. "I really hadn't thought of that. I guess we'll have to give him up. Or . . . wait! You can raise him."

"I'm serious, Mom," Merry said.

"I'm serious too, Meredith. If my doctor didn't think I could do this, I wouldn't do this. And by the way, both of you, Mallory too, can you tell me how old Grandma Gwen is?"

"She's, um, seventy-six," said Mallory.

"And how old is your dad's sister, Aunt Jenny?"

"She's thirty . . . I don't know. She's thirty or so," Mallory said, sitting down with a weary thump and pulling on her hoodie.

"She's thirty-five. Twelve years younger than your dad. She just got married last fall, and she's having a baby next spring too. How old was your grandmother when Aunt Jenny was born?"

"I never thought about that," Mally admitted. "Grandma would have been past forty when Aunt Jenny was born."

"So, see? There was another case like this in national history."

"What are we going to name him?"

"Arness."

"NO!" the girls shouted at her.

Merry ventured, "That's stupid. How about a nice name? Like Justin?"

"Every second kid is named Justin. How about Sascha?"

"How about fruitcake?" Mallory asked. "Just think of a normal name."

Meaningfully, then, Mallory turned to Merry. "Hey. Let's not tire Mom out. You don't have practice. Let's go for a run."

"I'm slobbing," Merry said.

"You don't want to miss a day, oh Varsity Queen. Let's go for a run."

"Ask Drew."

"I'm asking you! We need to run over to Grandma's and pick some stuff up!"

"What stuff?" Merry asked. "Plus, Grandma's is four miles one way! It's thirty-five degrees outside and it's gonna snow!"

With a tiny fist, Mallory popped Merry on the arm. "Come on, cheerleaders-are-athletes! Let's go get dressed!"

"Okay, *okay!*" Merry rubbed her arm. She shot off to grab her sweats, knowing by then that there was more that Mallory needed than a running partner. But not to give up too easily, she called back over her shoulder, "Mom! You should give Mal some of that moisturizer! Her chin's dry!"

Mallory immediately covered her chin.

"I know what makes a chin look like that, Mal-o-mar," Campbell said placidly.

Yikes! Mallory had put on a gob of moisturizer and some of Merry's corpse concealer too!

"Who's the boy?"

"Mom, it's not a boyfriend."

"Then why are you kissing him? You're not even fourteen."

"In a week, Mom!"

"Almost two weeks. And you're so, so not allowed to date."

"It's Eden's brother. He goes to Boston Flanders. He got a scholarship for Latin."

"How old is he?"

"He's sixteen. Just turned. He's a sophomore."

"Okay," Campbell said. "I'm still not on board. You can just get some cereal or a piece of cornbread, missy, before you go running. You're getting too thin. I told you that before Thanksgiving. And you haven't listened."

"I'm just changing, Mom."

"I'll say. I saw you changing your clothes into that nifty black-and-burgundy sweater before you went out with Eden the other night. Was that boy along?"

"Cooper, Mom. And yes. With about sixteen little sisters and cousins."

Cooper was home for Christmas too—until January 7—because private schools gave longer breaks. Although Mally had seen him only a couple of times, there was enough electricity between them to power all the lights on the square. When Mally went with him and Eden and their older sister Bly to take all the little Cardinal kids to a Disney movie, she and Cooper slipped out for popcorn and slipped back into two seats apart from the group. Once again, Mallory went home with her chin the same shade of pink as her lips.

"Groups are okay," Campbell said. "It wasn't more than kissing, was it?"

"No!" Mallory yelled, feeling like she was lying, because Cooper had stroked her neck and back and pressed her close to him in a way that felt wrong but also good and was, Mally knew, not really anything out of bounds—but which she also could not stop thinking about. "No way! Can't I have a crush like a normal human being? Don't you think it's about time?"

"Actually, I do," Campbell said. "And if he's like Eden, he's probably a good boy. And when you're fifteen, he won't be too old for you. It's tough to be younger than the other ones in your grade. And younger than you want to be."

"I'm not. Not really," Mallory said. "Just . . . for this."

"Well, just watch it, Mallory. Emotions run right over your brains."

"I know, Mom," Mallory said. "I really know. My head is spinning."

"Everyone's head spins. He's a good-looking boy. A real barn burner. Keep your feet on the ground."

"Why did you ask me if you already knew? When did you see Cooper?"

"I get around. I saw him in the stands last fall when Eden played. Before Halloween. Very handsome."

"Oh. God. Okay."

They both stopped to laugh at the sound of Merry muttering as she searched the wreck of a closet for two gloves that matched a hat to pull on. The run would put her in a better mood. There was a crash as Merry muttered that she'd finally located her lost water bottles and belt clips.

Campbell kissed Mallory on both cheeks. "Do you hate me about the baby too?"

"Hate you? We don't hate you. We were just scared it was too much for you. *We're* too much for you."

"No, you're not," Campbell said. "Kids! You have to feel guilty about everything. Go on and run. Decide what you want to do for your birthday. I have an idea, but you might think it's stupid."

"Try me."

"Come *on*!" Merry shouted from the hall.

"I'm coming!" Mally called back. "What, Mom?"

"If it snows, how about a sleigh ride? A big sleigh that holds maybe sixteen people? And a team?"

"Okay, we'll use our team of horses."

"Actually, it was Julie Barnes's brother who got stitched up at the ER last month. She was so glad we got to him before her kid got hurt, she came in and suggested we could use hers anytime. She owns the big natural garden store and pumpkin patch out by

Deptford? And then maybe we'll have some chili and stuff out there in the garage and some music, and you can have a few more people over. Not like last year."

"Please not like last year!"

"But a few. How's that?"

"That would really actually be kind of . . ."

"Romantic," said Campbell.

"I wasn't thinking that," Mallory said.

"You were too."

Mally asked, "Mom, what are you . . . psychic?"

UNDER A WING

You're too thin, Mallory," Grandma Gwenny said, once they'd peeled off their layers. "Let me get you something to eat."

"We just ran four miles, Grandma," Mallory said. "If I eat now, I'll puke."

"What's wrong with you?"

"She's in love," Merry said maliciously.

"I'm not in love!" Mallory snapped. She punched Merry again.

"She's so in love, and if you hit me once more, I'll kick you until you can't walk. These legs are lethal weapons."

"Your mouth is a lethal weapon," Mallory answered, but then softened. "Did you hear Mom's idea for our party?"

"Yes."

"Didn't you like it, Ster?"

"I thought it was dumb and babyish. Other than that, it's okay."

"A sleigh ride sounds nice," Mallory said, picturing herself tucked in a big robe with Cooper's arm around her. It would be a group, after all. But maybe Mom was so right. What would Cooper see in a fourteen-year-old? Cooper could have any girl he wanted. "And food and a party afterward."

"It sounds nice to you because you are an unsophisticated person," Merry said.

"It sounds dumb to you because you don't even have a pretend boyfriend."

"Only because I want it that way."

"Only because most people think cheerleaders are bizarre."

Grandma returned with steaming slices of apple crisp, folded on a tray, with a small dish of pure maple sugar next to each one. She'd laid cloth napkins under the plates so they'd be warm. Grandma always did everything right, not slap dash. She dressed up for her food-delivery runs to "senior citizens," because she said her cheerful appearance was part of the good of the experience for her clients. So when she frowned at them, the twins went silent.

"Girls!" Grandma Gwenny said. "You never argue this way."

"We do now!" Merry told her, and Mallory realized that it was true. Since she'd been keeping secrets, they had been fighting more—more than the constant teasing that was a pleasure to both of them.

"I don't want to fight, really fight, Mer," Mally said. "But I'm in a bad way. I have stuff I need to talk over. I can't keep it to myself anymore. It's serious."

"What?" Merry asked, genuinely concerned.

"What if your best friend was in true trouble, and there was nothing you could do about it? Nothing?" Mallory asked.

"What if your best friend was in true trouble, and there was nothing you could do about it?" Merry replied.

"I'm talking about Eden."

"I'm talking about Kim."

And then they spilled the secrets: Kim's dangerous friends and her drinking, her horrible sabotage of Crystal and possibly Merry, her sadness as deep as a well. Meredith's eyes widened as she listened to the truth about Eden and the lion. But she wasn't truly shocked. "A part of me knew it wasn't a symbol," she said. "But I couldn't bear knowing the truth. And as for her being ... like us, I've known that for a long time." She got up from the bench on the opposite side of Grandma's neat, planked Amish table and sat down next to Mallory on her bench.

"And I can't stand that Kim did this to Crystal. I know we should tell the police," Mallory said.

Grandma said, "Would Kimberly end up in a juvenile facility? Would that make her better or make her worse?"

All three of them sat silently. Then Grandma Gwenny got up and cut two more slices of the apple crisp.

"So, say we try to work with Kim?" Mallory answered. "What happens to Eden? I can beg her and I can keep the secret, but I can't really influence her."

"Can you really influence anyone?" Grandma asked.

"But what if she gets truly hurt? What if she hurts people?" Mallory asked, devouring her second piece in the safety of her grandmother's kitchen—where neither romance nor pain could intrude—and reaching for Merry's unfinished crust.

"We were responsible for a death," Merry said. "And if people knew all about David and us, we would be treated like the village crazies."

"Anno," Mallory said, taking Merry's hand, using the twin language that meant she understood. "I'm sorry you had to keep this inside."

"I'm sorry for you. And remember, Eden is my friend too."

"And Kim's mine. Not like you, but we have a long history."

"I don't know why I didn't feel safe telling you about Kim. Or asking about Edie. I guess it makes it real. I didn't dream the connection, but I knew."

"We're getting used to who we are, and what we are, and it just flows in, I guess. Maybe it won't always be in dreams," Mally suggested. "It would be better if I didn't have to black out, or at least so people noticed. Did you black out, Grandma?" Their grandmother shook her head.

Merry asked Mallory, "Are you getting used to it?"

"I was before . . . this, with Eden. Every time I think I can handle it and live with it, it raises the stakes," Mallory said.

"Why doesn't Eden hide in her yard? I guess that's obvious. She'd scare all those little kids."

"Not all those kids even know about her. But I don't think she meant to hurt the hunter. He shot at her!" said Mallory. "But then, who wouldn't shoot at a white mountain lion up here? Let's assume all I can do for Eden is talk and hope and pray. What can we do for Kim?"

"I felt terrible when I lied and told her that there were surveillance cameras in the suiting-up area. But she already had a guilty conscience. That's why she quit. She didn't say why she simply had to make varsity this year. She just said she had to. And then she quit."

They both looked at Gwenny.

"If we can't say what we know to someone, what do we say?" Merry asked.

"I don't think it makes anything worse to talk about it," Grandma Gwenny said. "Don't you think Kim's probably expecting you to ask? Don't you think Eden is expecting you to ask, Mallory, after the incident?"

The twins nodded.

"I could go to the Jellicos. But I'm so scared to do that, Grandma. Like maybe I'll see him. Can there be angry ghosts?" Grandma looked away. Merry knew that meant it was indeed possible. "If he died not knowing what happened? All I saw was this flash of white, and now, of course . . ."

"You know what that was," Mallory said. "That's why you saw her following me, when you were at Neely's. She wouldn't have let David hurt you."

"So Eden saved my life. Is she coming to our party?"

"Of course," Mally said.

"I want to thank her for what she did for me."

"She already knows. And she's pretty shy."

"Okay," Merry said quietly. "Well, I'm going to go see Kim tonight. I have an idea, but Coach might not go for it. Let's get running."

"Oh," Grandma Gwenny said, "I think you're going to need to ski."

The girls glanced outside. The snow was already more than four inches deep.

"Let's get you home. The big car has good snow tires," Grandma said.

"Aren't you scared to drive in the snow?" Merry asked. "Because most . . ."

"Most old ladies are?"

"Grandma, you aren't old!" Merry said, blushing and hugging Gwenny. "You have a daughter who's only thirty-five! You were a mother when you were over forty."

"Well, I'm not the only one," Grandma said. "Isn't it wonderful? A little boy? She's thinking of naming him Arness, after her family, but Arnie isn't that modern a nickname. I'll bet she names him Owen Campbell. I know she likes the name Owen."

"When did Mom tell you?" Mally asked, as they got into Grandma's compact little SUV, the one Grandpa called her "Plant-mobile."

"She only really told us today," added Merry.

Gwenny smiled. "She didn't tell me, of course. You know what I see. Healthy babies in the future. My poor sister was seeing the babies who wouldn't live, seeing all the deaths."

"So the baby will be fine? Mom will be fine?" Merry asked eagerly.

"Why, yes," Gwenny said. "Whatever did you think?"

SONG OF JOY, SONG OF SORROW

O n the night of her Christmas concert, Mallory glanced out her bedroom window and saw that snow was falling. She sighed. It had been the only thing lacking. Now the night would be perfect.

She'd spent a full half hour getting dressed. Cooper was coming, and Mally hadn't quite worked up the courage to ask him to her party. But this night, this magical night of music and soft wintry welcoming, she planned to invite him.

Miss Yancy insisted each girl wear black and white.

So Mallory wore her new long black velvet skirt, Campbell's white satin shirt, and a shrug sweater she had found just hours before. It turned up in a package left on the porch.

The makeup nearly did her in. She wouldn't master eyeliner until she was thirty, if ever. She had to swab off the excess with baby oil four times and start over. This time, at least the mascara stayed put.

Mally knew the origin of the sweater.

A few days earlier, Mallory had noticed Eden knitting something in black mohair. It was during the afternoon Eden agreed to join Mallory for a full week's orgy of *General Hospital* tapes, which took about an hour and a half to watch back-to-back. When Mally asked about the project, Eden simply said she never really knew what things would be until she got going. And it was true that these days, she was always knitting—even during team meetings. It was like a nervous tic. ("We go through a lot of mittens," Eden told Mallory. "And I make socks for James. He loves the homemade ones.") But Mallory could tell Eden was using knitting to calm herself.

As she set up her old VCR with a tape, Mally explained that she had decided to watch all the *General Hospital* episodes in order, as far back as she had, which was 1983. "There'll be gaps, of course, but it's like reading an epic poem," she told Eden.

"Or like an epic bore," Eden said.

"Be nice. See how miserable Luke is? He thinks of Laura all the time, but she hides from him. I don't know why she's hiding from him. She just does. I don't even know why she left. He's running around thinking she's dead and she's right in that town they live in. I bought these tapes from our neighbor, and she didn't have any before 1983."

"Maybe she ran away because she was too sad to stay. Maybe she couldn't have the life she wanted, and that's why," Eden said.

"Edes, that's a good reason if you're like . . . thirty-five."

"It's a good reason no matter what age you are," Eden said. "I'm starting to think it's a better idea all the time. If bad things happen to you, you belong somewhere else."

"Eden, I know what that means."

Eden had set her knitting aside, but she picked it up again, to give herself something to fiddle with. Finally she said, "I know you're not stupid. Just because I haven't come out and talked about what happened up behind the reservoir and why you came up . . ."

"I didn't want to make you talk about it. I didn't know if it went out of your mind after you . . . were you again."

"To answer that, no, but it's like a dream, like a ghost memory. But you know, I won't let anyone hurt you. I won't let anyone hurt me or any of mine. And if I have to be out there, I'm sick of hiding in a hole until midnight when I'm starving."

"Would it help if I brought you food?"

"Like pizza?" Eden collapsed on the couch. "Oh, Mallory. We're a pair! Only if it has meatballs. I'm not a little house cat! I have to get out of this, Mally. Some way."

"Promise me one thing," Mally said. "Promise you'll tell me first."

Eden was silent for a long time, bent over her needles. "Okay," she said. "Only you. Not my brother. He's all paranoid about this."

"He has a right to be, Eden!"

Eden didn't answer. Finally, she said, "I think Merry's right. You're sick. If these shows grow on you, they grow like fungus."

"Come to my concert," Mally said, for the second time that day.

"I . . . can't come," Eden said. "Will Miss Yancy record it?"

"They'll make DVDs."

"I'll get one," Eden told her. She got up and gave Mallory a hug. "I have to run. Tell Luke I'm heartbroken for him."

"Why can't you come?"

"Mallory. You know. I'm busy for the next few nights. I'll come to your party, though."

It was sweet for a junior to come to a freshman's party, but Mally knew why Eden, who loved choral music, was missing the concert. She would have to sing her heart out, worrying all the while.

"Will you be careful? Those kids out there, they saw you clearly. You knew that, didn't you?"

Eden sighed. She said, "I can't believe I'm saying this to anyone but family, but when I'm . . . that way, Mal, I'm me but not me. I only sense danger to one of my own. You don't know how it is to be trapped!"

"I do know. I have a destiny of my own. And if it's your destiny . . ."

"I'm trying to change that! I have to!"

"Does James know?"

"Only that I have to hide the truth about him and me from my family. I've told him that we have a legend about a white lion. He thinks it's charming, like folklore. Not even all my brothers and sisters know. Even my father pretends he doesn't. He feels guilty, I think. And yet, I still get in trouble with him for missing school if it happens when it's not on a weekend. There's not one part of it that's even a little fair. I don't even believe that my grandmother saw me the instant I was born and knew I was the successor."

"My grandmother knew about us the minute she saw us too."

"Your whole problem is different. I can't prove I'm useful. I really think my parents and brothers and sisters and cousins will be fine. The farm's doing great. Grandma's going to be in a story in the *New York Times* for her beading. I don't buy it. It's like being a weird nun without a deity."

Mally handed Eden her coat. She said, "But there must be a reason. Or you wouldn't change at all. I don't want what I was given, but there must be a reason. It's part of me. I wouldn't know about you or how to protect you otherwise. I wouldn't know that mountain lions ate pizza!" Eden laughed, but Mallory continued, in a serious vein. "You've saved lives. Merry owes her life to you."

"Tell her I just gave her one of mine. I have nine, you know." Eden's eyes brightened with tears. "I didn't want to hurt that boy, David. But he was the predator, Mal. David was doing more than you know. I never dug . . . I never tried to find what's really down there. But someone will, someday. I couldn't let him hurt Merry!"

"How much is it worth to save a life?"

"It's worth a lot," Eden said. "But is it worth my life? Is it worth me living alone forever, never knowing love, growing old, never having babies? Watching my sisters have families while I knit and make ornamental headdresses and potions? You can be free!"

"You're never free if you can see the future, Eden. Yes, I can get married and even move away. But I won't ever be free."

"I want to do right," Eden said. "But maybe it won't matter."

Her words came back to Mallory as she dressed for her

concert, slipping the soft black sweater over her shoulders. It fit as though, well, as though it had been made for her. She sent a silent prayer for Eden's safety and straightened the sweater and the length of velvet ribbon she'd tied around the neck of her blouse.

When she came down into the kitchen, her uncle Kevin asked, "My eyes confuse me; this can't be Mallory?"

"Oh, yes," Campbell said. "We've got quite the young lady now."

They all piled into vans and cars, and though Christmas was still days away, the light snow falling made it feel as though the holiday was this very night.

Before the concert, Mallory peeked out from the wings and was almost embarrassed. It was like one of Merry's home meets—all the aunts and uncles and cousins. But tonight, they included Aunt Jenny and her new husband, their baby, due in April . . . just like . . . just like her little brother. It made her proud, looking up there at all their smiling Yankee faces, still ruddy with cold.

Something turned over in her heart. She realized that time would change this picture.

One day, Grandpa Walker, who was ninety-two, would no longer be among them. Adam would soon be a teenager. She counted twenty members of her family—all there for her. Campbell was beaming in a long satin tunic that showed her big belly, and there had been much laughter at the house earlier as she and Aunt Jenny compared tummies. "I look so old!" Campbell mourned.

No matter what, tonight Mallory was a lucky girl, almost a woman. She felt the ache and joy of growing older.

The concert choir sang a series of winter songs and carols, including an electrified version of "Deck the Halls" and "Winter Wonderland."

When the time came for her duet, she easily sang the alto part of the German version of "Lo, How a Rose E'er Blooming," with Alice Haslanger singing the soprano melody.

As the audience applauded, Miss Yancy went wild.

"Girls," she told the Cantabiles, "that was the most beautiful version of that I've ever heard from my students. Keep this up and I'll take up my colleagues' offer to come to Italy and sing one day in Florence!" The girls rustled and giggled with the potential excitement. "At least we'll win first at state in March!"

The whole audience, hundreds of people, stayed for cookies and punch afterward. But as Mally thanked people for the comments on her new appearance and her never-before-heard singing voice, she noticed only one figure break away from the crowd. And then he was beside her, his dark hair shining and smelling of the old lavender tonic his grandfather had worn, and which would have smelled silly on anyone but Cooper.

"Hey," she said. "Mr. Cardinal."

"I knew Brynn meant a dark wing, but I didn't think it meant a lark," he said.

"You're such a flirt!"

"I heard rumors from my sister of a New Year's Eve birthday party to which I'm not invited," he said.

"You wouldn't want to come to a fourteen-year-old's sleigh ride," Mallory told him. "Or would you?"

"There are fourteen-year-olds and there are fourteen-year-olds," Cooper said. "Some are just too hard to resist."

And Mallory wished again that the picture of this night would last forever.

RECKONING AND RECOGNITION

RECKONING AND RECOGNITION

Kim cheered for the varsity boys' basketball game the night before the twins' party.

It was a big deal, the holiday tournament, and Merry had to admire Pam Door for giving up her spot and being "in" on Kim's sudden reelevation to varsity, on a part-time basis.

It *had* taken Merry's best powers to convince Coach why Kim needed to be reinstated, to persuade her that Kim hadn't spurned the honor of being named to varsity. Coach, although she was strict, had watched Kim wither over the long months since David died, her cheerful enthusiasm turn to purely mechanical skill. Coach had always believed that cheerleading was as much about building spirits as solid pyramids. Meredith suspected that Coach chose Kim in the first place not only because she was good but because Kim needed the emotional boost. As for Merry, she felt as though she'd made varsity all over again. She and Pam would give up a fourth of their games each, so Kim could cheer for the rest of the year on varsity.

"What's become of cutthroat competition?" Coach asked. "Well, I guess your values are better than mine!"

Meredith knew that wasn't true. Under her bluster, Coach was proud of her girls.

"I'll be cheering in college anyhow! I have a scholarship," Pam told Coach Everson. "What are a few extra games?"

Only Meredith knew the real reason why Kim had been so desperate.

And she had promised on her heart not to tell.

To break the news about her plan, Merry had to go to the Jellicos' house. Nervous to the point of nausea, she waited until Bonnie opened the door—Bonnie, who'd been like a second mom to her until last year. Bonnie's blond hair now was the color of burned paper. She didn't even bother with a little lipgloss. If anything, Bonnie, three years younger than Merry's mom, looked ten years older. The house was still a shrine, with even more pictures of David than right after he died.

Like a little ghost, Kim appeared and led Merry up the back stairs to her room.

A few moments later, without Merry even having to ask, Kim was crying, harder and harder.

"I never thought it would really hurt Crystal. Never! I thought she'd mess up her footwork just enough so I'd look better. She's so flexible and she can do anything! I didn't even really know if it would work. I just read about it on some blog. And even after I did it, after I put the tape on, I wanted to run out there and stop it. But if I got expelled, it would be the real end."

"What do you mean, Kim?" Merry asked.

"It's all me," Kim said.

"Huh?"

"It's all me now. I have to be perfect. I have to be everything to them now. I have to make up for . . ."

"To make up for David."

"Yes."

"They don't really feel like that."

"But they do, Merry! You don't know what happened."

"Do you want to tell me?"

"My dad counts on me to keep . . . Mom alive. . . ."

"What do you mean, Kim?"

"Two months after David died, Mom took an overdose. She saved up all the sleeping pills the doctors gave her and she took them all. Your mom doesn't even know. Dad was so ashamed."

"Ashamed?"

"Yes! That's how he is, Merry. He drove her all the way to the city, even though she was barely conscious."

"No way!"

"He took her to an ER there, so no one here would know. He thought we would be ruined forever. After David dying and then my mom."

"He drove her for an hour and a half? She could have died."

"So when I told her that I'd made varsity, it was just two months later. And she was happy, Merry. Not happy like before David, but almost excited. About me. It was the first time. Because David was the best. . . ."

"What do you mean?"

"He was popular and good-looking, and I just wasn't ever as good as he was," Kim said. "It was like they were . . . not just completely devastated that David died, but they got the leftover kid."

"Stop it, Kim."

"I heard Dad say it," Kim told her. "I heard Dad. Right after David died. He said, all we have left is Kim. He said, 'Do you know how that feels, Bonnie? I had the most wonderful son on earth. My pride. My name! And now we have our cheerleader!'"

Merry pulled Kim close, her tiny body suddenly large enough to comfort someone thirty pounds heavier and four inches taller than she.

Another secret Merry could never speak. Shame on them. Even if out of his mind with grief, how could anyone say such a thing, much less feel it? How could Mr. Jellico, even though he was a professor, feel that Kim wasn't as good as David? Her parents might be a pain, but they would never, not ever think less of her than of Mallory, or Adam. They were all . . . cherished. That, Merry realized, made the gift bearable.

Despite her fears, Kim's need and gratitude were so great that Merry let Kim talk her into staying over. She barely slept, believing that any second she'd wake to David's eyes in the darkness, blazing in maniac glee, the way they had on the ridge. Where else would he be, except here, where candles burned in his memory, where his senior picture had been transformed into an oil painting four times its size, where pale, haggard Bonnie cleaned his room and laundered his clothes as though David would walk in the door at any moment?

Where his mother had tried to die to be with him?

In the morning, Bonnie drove both of them to practice on her way to work. As she left, Bonnie said softly, "Say hi to your mom, Merry. Tell her congrats about the baby. I . . . I wish I had another chance."

"I will," Merry said. She took a deep breath and said, "Bonnie, Mom misses you. She loved working with you. She only took the ER job because she needed the money. For the baby. And she's going to medical school."

Bonnie, a distant look in her eyes, said, "She is? I'm glad. I never returned her calls."

Merry longed to say, "You do have another chance, Bonnie! She's right here." But she knew what Bonnie meant.

That night at halftime, Merry rushed out onto the floor to do something she'd only ever tried in practice and only once in competition—a lib on top of a pyramid formed by four on the bottom and Kim and Libby Entwhistle supporting her balanced on the legs of the four below. Kim and Merry would first do a tumbling pass to the center of the floor, a walkover to a round-off, into three front handsprings, and then up Merry would go, to pull an outsized red-and-green pom-pom from her sleeve and wave madly while she extended one leg. She waited for the opening words, "Green light! That's right!" As soon as she saw Kim start toward her, she couldn't help but grin. With Kim's face alight, Merry forgot everything. Muscle memory took over as she watched Kim cavort like a kid on a trampoline.

As Merry stood on the pyramid, she hoped that Danny Blinkhorn, who'd dumped Trevor at Thanksgiving, might be looking her way. He wasn't, but she saw something else: She saw Bonnie on her feet with tears in her eyes, and David's father—*Kim's* father—clapping his hands.

As they rushed into their dance, picking up their bells for the routine to "Jingle Bell Rock," Kim whispered, "My mom's looking at me! At me! Since David's been gone, and especially since . . . what I told you, my mom hasn't even seen me. Not when I stay out all night. Never."

"Are you happy?"

"I'll never be happy like you, Merry. You can't be if you lose someone. But I'm as happy as I can be. Because of you."

"Well, do I get a present for that?"

Kim looked puzzled. "You mean a birthday present?" They lined up and waited for the opening notes.

"Yes, sure. Call it that. I want you to promise me just one thing. That you'll never go to the ravine again. That you'll hang with us again. Or at least try to." Kim looked away. "Kimmie? I hate to guilt trip you, but I gave up one fourth of my season. That's a lot."

"I always wanted to!" Kim burst out. "I didn't think you wanted me!"

"Well, now you know. I'll take that as yes?"

"Yes! Sure! Anything!" Kim cried, and they rushed out onto the floor.

ON THE NIGHT THEY WERE BORN

ON THE NIGHT THEY WERE BORN

M allory snuggled under Cooper's arm and thought, *What a difference from last New Year's Eve.*

The sleigh slushed over the snow around the reservoir. Merry had cajoled Danny Blinkhorn to come "just as a friend," and was gossiping with Drew and Pam Door. Kim was there with Brice, a new boyfriend from Deptford but seemingly very nice. Everybody spread rumors about the boys from Deptford, but Mallory was sick of rumors.

She knew there were already rumors about Cooper and her. And she knew they weren't nice.

For her part, she wasn't ever going to believe again anything she couldn't prove with her own eyes—or in her case, the eyes inside her mind. The Barnes' team of beautiful, mild-eyed Clydesdales trotted for an hour among the trees festooned with snow. Cooper tickled Mally's nose with the end of her scarf. He did nothing in the way of PDA, but there was very much a sense that she was Cooper's girl. For that hour, all was right with the world.

Julie surprised them with hot cider when they got back to the barn. Dressed in feather-light parkas (Merry's baby blue and Mallory's bright red) made of some space-age fabric, and matching lined boots of Australian suede, the girls looked as shiny as they felt. Grandma Gwen had crocheted matching caps and mittens, but for Mallory the best gift was left on her porch. At the last minute, Drew gave Mallory six of his grody old shirts, tied with a ribbon. A peace offering. The bundle included one new T-shirt from the mall that read "Cheerleaders Give It Their All," which made Campbell's eyes narrow when she saw it, although she decided Drew meant it as no more than a gentle jest. Even Adam had come up with a certificate for the twins' iPods. With all the little gifts from relatives trickling in all week, they were feeling that "little Christmas" way they sometimes did having a birthday that came just after a major holiday.

Back at their house, a few other friends joined them for a tub of Campbell's special Italian beef. By the time they got there, she was ladling the steaming beef onto generous slices from huge, crusty loaves. Mallory, the first in the door, noticed that Campbell wore a tight, glittery black sweater—no attempt to hide her belly tonight. Rushing up to her mother, she patted her sibling-to-be.

Before coming in, Mallory had eagerly counted the cars in front: There was Eden's old truck and the Range Rover that belonged to the Brents, which meant that Will and his older brother, Rob, were there. Just as she and Cooper, with Merry in the backseat, pulled

into the drive, Neely Chaplin hopped out of her parents' Beemer—
a little ad for Clothes That Counted, from her Italian sweater to
her Finnish boots. But Mallory didn't mind: Neely mouthed the
words "so hot" when she set eyes on Cooper. As Mallory helped
her mother put the sandwiches on plates with chips, Eden suddenly
appeared from inside the house, wearing a long red shirt belted over
a red skirt and boots, with the same infinitesimal braids with beads
in her hair she'd worn on the night of the powwow. "Hi!" she said,
pulling Mallory aside and giving her a birthday hug. She pointed to
her braids. "Some of these have a mind of their own. I guess I didn't
really have my mind on putting them in tonight."

As the boys began to eat and the music began to play, Eden shyly
and secretly showed Mallory her left hand. "I want to show you,"
she said. A tiny diamond winked in a white gold setting on her
ring finger.

"You're . . . engaged?" Mallory's world seemed to screech to a
stop.

"No, it's a promise ring. For after I finish at least a year of
college. James is getting his Master's. He had an emergency tonight
with one of his kids who had to come back out into the field so he
couldn't come." Mallory was relieved. She wouldn't have known
how to look at a guy who was seven years older at a kid party. And
especially now.

"Edes, do you think this is smart? Has your mom seen it?"

"Are you kidding?" Eden asked sharply. "I can't wear it in
school or at home, but I know he loves me. That's all that matters.
It's beautiful, isn't it?"

"Nothing's more beautiful, or terrible, than love. I heard you say that, huh?" Mallory murmured.

"Eden," Cooper said, taking Eden's hand before she could slip it behind her back, "nice Christmas present."

"It's just a friendship ring," Eden said.

"I hope it is, for your sake," Cooper said sadly. "I don't want to be the bad guy, sis, but James . . ."

"James doesn't know anything about it. About me."

"I was going to say," Cooper went on smoothly, "James should know better than to be giving rings to a high school girl."

"He doesn't think of me like that. I could easily be out at my age, except for my so-called delicate condition that kept me out of school for a year! He thinks of me as the woman he loves."

"That would be heavy talk even if you weren't who you are," Cooper said.

"I don't intend to be who I am, Cooper," Eden said quietly.

"That's the first time you said it straight out," Cooper told her. He pressed his lips together. "At least promise to pray and fast about this."

"What does he mean?" asked Mallory, whose mood was sinking like the balloons on the ceiling in the warmth of the garage.

"He means shut myself up in the longhouse and not eat for three days until I feel totally woozy and guilty for ever wanting my own life," Eden said bitterly. "Mally, I'm sorry. I have to leave."

"Eden, it can wait."

"I just don't feel like being at a party. Even yours." Eden kissed Mally's cheek. "Happy birthday."

Cooper said, "When she gets like this, it's better to listen to her."

"I wish it were you, Cooper!" Eden snapped.

Cooper said nothing. Then he whispered, "This isn't the time or the place, Eden. But you do get to be the boss of the clan."

"All the young people will run away to the cities, like Bly. I can have a job, but I don't have to! The clan will always take care of me."

"You love so many things, Eden. Art and words . . ." Mally began.

"Let Raina be the next shape-shifter!" Mallory had never seen Eden so angry. She stomped off and the other kids stared. Sensing something but not what, Tim put the music on loud. Campbell brought the cake into the garage. It was all covered with chocolate musical notes.

"We figured your cheer dances are music and now Mallory's singing," Campbell explained. "It's my last gasp of being a good mother and doing the baking thing. You guys get to eat hot dogs until the end of March."

Everyone sang "Happy Birthday," and Mallory's mood began to bubble again. As Campbell cut the cake, Tim added, "I happen to know that there's one more gift for Mallory."

He smiled at Cooper Cardinal.

Cooper was too dark to really blush, but his cheeks looked as though someone had laid a little finger of fire along each cheekbone.

"Anyone who can't stand ugly sounds should leave now," he said, to a murmur of laughter. Tim brought Cooper a stool and gave him his own old guitar, the one Tim had had since college. "I learned to play a little at school and this song has exactly two chords, so Mallory's dad was nice enough to be in on this with me. And my dad was nice enough to teach me this song, which was old when he was young. It's by John Sebastian. You probably never heard of him, but it's a great song. Be patient with my lousy guitar playing." Cooper spent a few minutes fiddling with Tim's guitar. "I'm pretending to tune it," he said with a laugh. Then, after a few opening notes, Cooper sang. His voice was higher and lighter than Mallory's.

"She's one of those girls who seems to come in the spring, and one look from her eyes makes you forget everything you had ready to say. And I saw her today. . . . A younger girl keeps rolling across my mind," Cooper sang. "No matter what he tried, he couldn't seem to leave her memory behind / In a few more years they'd call them 'right for each other' / But why? If he waited, he'd die / A younger girl keeps rolling across my mind . . . ."

Mallory had never cried in public except on the day she "heard" Meredith call out in fear for her life. Now two fat tears rolled down her cheeks, and she didn't even bother to wipe them away. Cooper's voice was as gentle and graceful as everything else about him. And it was just such a sweet, yearning song—so much of what she felt. She didn't notice the other girls glancing at her under their lashes with envy. She only saw Cooper. When he finished, Mallory gave him a light kiss on the cheek, in front of everyone.

Merry paused to whisper to Mally, without a trace of sarcasm, "That was completely the most romantic thing I ever heard, Ster."

Then she gathered a crowd around her as she began opening presents.

Mallory was walking on air.

Campbell, however, had both feet on the ground.

"Meredith's right. That was beautiful," she told Cooper, as he handed Tim's guitar over to her. "That is one of the sweetest songs ever written. I was probably Adam's age or younger when I first heard it."

"Thank you, Mrs. Brynn."

"Mallory is very innocent."

"No, she's not that," Cooper said. *Enjoy this moment,* Mallory thought then, as she watched Campbell's face morph from disbelief to outright anger. *You won't be out after six at night again until you're twenty.* "I'm not talking about boys. If I were going to take advantage of a girl, like that, it wouldn't be Eden's . . . whatever . . . Eden's protégé. I'm more afraid of Eden than I am of you, no offense. I mean Mally's older in ways other than years."

To Mallory's relief, the other kids had drifted away. Campbell considered Cooper's words. "That's possible. What she saw last year changed her."

"I mean she's sensitive to people."

"I accept that. She's mature in that way. But she's only fourteen."

"Please kill me," Mallory whispered. "Mom, Cooper's leaving in two days. I don't think he wants to run off and marry me before morning. We're friends. Can you save the lecture?"

"I'm not lecturing," Campbell said. "I just want him to know that Shakespeare was right. 'These violent delights have violent ends'."

"Oh. It's Shakespeare now! Great. I'm not going to commit suicide either! Mom, please! It's a party!"

Cooper said, "I know how Mallory feels, Mrs. Brynn, and that it's unusual for her. The first time. No! Not that kind of first time! The first time she cared about a guy. I wouldn't . . . I respect that and I respect Mallory."

Campbell looked hard at Cooper. She said softly, "Okay. I believe you. Don't let me be wrong." She began to walk away, toward Meredith and Neely, who had been eavesdropping ferociously. Then she turned back. "That was a tremendously touching birthday gift, Cooper."

Later that night, they stood in the snow, and Cooper tilted Mallory's chin up to kiss her good night, promising to come to see her before he left.

"You were great with Mom. No one ever says boo to her."

"I was sweating the whole time," Cooper admitted. "Now I know where you get your personality!"

THE ESCAPE

Slowly, the residents of Ridgeline slogged through the last of the cold.

Skiers were thrilled that the snow stayed deep, with a new coat of light powder every few days. No one could remember a time when more than two feet of snow had stayed on the ground for two full months without going slushy and gray.

The Brynn twins took out their cross-country skis and cajoled their father into giving them new boots from the store, since they had outgrown theirs for the first time in three years. Out in the country, near their uncle Kevin's house, they skied all over the farm fields and up and down the slight hullocks, returning to see Aunt Kate and their little cousins drained and sweaty as they never were from running. She gave them pumpkin-spiced tea and cookies and oranges. They skied the Cardinals' land and tried the small hills.

But nothing could tire Mallory enough to make her stop thinking.

Each day, Mallory did everything but remove the mailbox and shake it upside down to see if a letter from Cooper would fall out.

None did.

She waited throughout January.

Why didn't Boston Flanders allow e-mail? The whole deal about how letter-writing, real letter-writing, was part of a classical education was a bunch of garbage! If he had e-mail, or even a cell phone, she could talk to Cooper once a day at least!

On Valentine's Day, instead of a sappy card, she got a postcard from Harvard. A guy with a red sweatshirt leaned against a column. The shirt read, "I Don't Really Go Here." On the back, Cooper had written, *My heart's in the highlands wherever I roam. I didn't make that up. Love, C.*

Eden said not to worry; boys simply didn't write long letters ever. She also counseled Mallory against sending any to Cooper.

"Make him wonder," Eden suggested. "Cooper thinks he's a real gift to women."

He is, Mallory thought.

She wrote Cooper pages of letters, then folded them away in the wooden keepsake box she'd had since she was ten. She never sent them.

Relentlessly, she did extra credit for English in hopes of getting straight A's. On long, brainless afternoons on the couch, she marched through 1984 and 1985 on *General Hospital,* marveling that she could have turned to any episode on any day of any week of any year before 1990 and been up to speed on the characters' lives within seconds. She also worked on her choir parts and solo for the spring concert.

Cantabile was more exciting now because, under pressure from Mallory, Meredith had joined after the basketball season ended and before the late spring competition season began. Merry had an extra study hall too, and Campbell assured Merry that, since she'd always had a sweet singing voice—a nice pure soprano—chorus would be an easy A or B. Miss Yancy was delighted. She quickly planned to showcase the twins in a duet for the spring concert of the old folk song "Green Leaves of Summer"—though Cantabile usually didn't do folk songs of any kind.

The words somehow made Mallory sad: *It was good to be young then / To be close to the earth / Now the green leaves of summer are calling me home.*

Cooper, come home, she thought, and then rebuked herself.

A year ago, she would have mocked her sister savagely for being America's number one priss. And now here she was, reliving one fifteen-minute kissing session over and over in her head until it was like a piece of paper she'd smudged and worn through with holes. She had to get over it.

With an abrupt turn of events, she almost did. She found herself bargaining with God that she'd give Cooper up if her soon-to-be-born little baby sibling would be okay.

Early in March, a month before her due date, Campbell began to have labor pains. Dr. Kellogg popped her into the hospital, where the pains subsided with medication. The twins and Adam went to the hospital to watch the little baby ("Not so little," said Dr. Kellogg) dancing on ultrasound. With the 3-D technology, they could see his squashed little alien monkey face.

"He looks like you," Adam told Merry.

"You look like that *now*," she replied placidly.

"I can't figure out what to name him," Campbell said.

"I can't figure out whether to put you on bed rest," said Dr. Kellogg, who then decided to do just that.

Relief and pandemonium reigned at home.

Every day after choral practice, the girls, Tim, and Adam went to visit their mom, who was receiving royal treatment and special treats from all her old friends, competing to give her backrubs and milk shakes. She was grumpy, however, until the librarian, a cousin of the Brynns, brought her a stack of novels that weren't even published yet. "You won't be doing a whole lot of this for the next few months," said Margie Bowen. "So you'd better stock up your head now." After that, every time the family came, with Chinese noodles or pizza—no-cheese-extra-onions—Campbell had her feet canted up and her nose in a book.

Even fussy Meredith used up all her clothing before there was a general decision to do the wash. The kids watched TV, normally forbidden on school nights, until Adam literally had circles under his eyes. Their little brother, whom they were already calling Buddy, had done them a good turn.

Eden was curiously busy—even more than usual.

Mallory had always felt a bit odd about asking her to do something, but now, when Mally reached out, Eden cheerfully but firmly put her off with a deft excuse.

Then one day, she asked Mally if she'd like her to drive her to the hospital to visit her mother and then go shopping. When she showed up, Mallory was stunned. Always glorious, Eden now seemed somehow burnished, as if the advent of spring had caused her to burst out of an outworn skin. Her hair was shinier, her skin glowing with deep rose tones under the gold. She'd cut her long hair, not short, but shorter, in a fashionable waterfall of long layers.

"Eden, you look like you've had a makeover," Campbell said, accepting a pot of crocuses Eden's mother had forced into bloom. "Thank you. And what's the cause of all this?"

"Nothing," Eden said brightly. "Just the end of a long winter. Mallory and I are going to go shop the spring sales."

"I'm not," Mally said. "After what I spent this last winter, it'll take me until next spring to buy the other half of my new-me wardrobe. If I even decide a new me is worth it."

"Practice starts in a week, doesn't it?" Campbell asked.

"Yes, and then nice clothes won't count at all," Mally said.

"For some things," Eden replied.

At the mall, Eden spent freely, on nightgowns and sundresses, new espadrille sandals and a big sun hat.

"Are you going on a cruise?" Mallory asked jokingly.

"No, but it's sunny in New Mexico," Eden answered.

"New Mexico?"

"I'm going with James," Eden said. "It's so fantastic I can't even breathe when I think about it. I fasted and I prayed. And I decided I have to follow my heart."

Mallory was floored. She cried, "Edie, what about your family and school? What about soccer and college? Have you asked your grandmother what would happen if James stayed with you, instead of you going with him?"

"It wouldn't be allowed! Do you think I want to leave little Honeybee and Raina and Tanisi and not see them grow up? Do you think I won't miss Cooper? That I'm ready to leave my mother and father? I'm not! It's my only chance."

"Why this time? Why not next time? You're so young, Eden. Eighteen is an adult by law. But not really. What if James isn't the one? What if you leave everyone and it goes wrong?"

"It won't go wrong."

Mallory pleaded, "No one thinks anything could go wrong when she's in love, Eden!"

"James was offered a full-time job in Santa Fe, with tuition benefits. I can take the HSED and start college. He says he'll come back for me, but what if he doesn't? A high school girl compared with the girls he'll meet at New Mexico State? He'll find someone else. And I'll be alone."

"Eden, don't you trust him? You're giving up your whole life for him, and you're afraid he'd find someone else?"

"Mallory, I'm just a kid from Ridgeline. I'm trapped in a life I can't stand anymore! At least if I lost James there, I'd still be free."

"What about me?" Mallory asked. "You and Drew are all I have."

"My Mallory, my little Mallory," Eden said. "You'll have a full and lovely life. You'll be happy. There are two of you. You have people to depend on who understand and care."

"So do you."

"No, Mallory. They depend on me. Now it's my turn."

Mallory had no idea what to say and less of what to do. Everything Eden said was right. Eden did owe way too much to her family. So much shouldn't be placed on one girl's shoulders, no matter how level or strong those shoulders were. But the danger to James and Eden in her dream came . . . from James and Eden. It wasn't turning on her family. It wasn't taking off at eighteen. Other people had done that and made lives for themselves. It was the heavy, unshakable sense of menace in the dream of James alone in the glade, beneath the cliff, the lion watching him from above—when something unspeakable happened.

SISTERS

SISTERS

That afternoon, when Mallory got out of Eden's car, she tried to wave good-bye brightly, but no sooner had she opened her backpack than a small white card fell out. This was like Edie. Anyone else would have sent a text message. But Eden would give Mallory something to hold in her hand, on all the long nights to come. She wanted to hold it against her heart. She wanted to rip it up.

Finally, she opened the envelope.

Mallory read:

> *Little Sister of the Dark,*
>
> *You know the love I have for you as a friend and as one like me. I know you understand this choice, but you fear for me, just as I would fear for you. Mallory, always choose your life no matter what your destiny is supposed to be. If I go soon enough,*

this destiny won't find me. And so, my dear friend,
I won't see you again for quite a while. If there is
a way that whatever I have been given lets me look
over you, I'll do that from afar, Little Sister of the
Dark. And I'll write to you from the high desert,
where I'll be safe with my love.

  XO,

  Eden

Mallory crushed the note in her hand.

No!

This was now! Not spring break, now!

What was Mallory to do with no notice?

Did she have even a night to spare? There was nothing she could do before morning, and until after church. Her father would be suspicious.

And so, she stayed awake until sleep weighed her down, only to wake in a sweat, shivering. She paced her room until she could no longer bear the sight of the walls, then padded softly down to the living room couch. Sleep came and went, with dreams that chased each other—dreams of wide brown eyes and almond golden eyes, teeth and claws and caves. At one A.M., Mallory sat up and texted Eden: ?4U. To her relief, Eden answered, 411? The information that Mallory wanted was simple: LEMENO WEN. *Please, please answer, Eden,* Mally thought.

And after a long interval, Eden wrote, PCKING. 2MORRO. Tomorrow.

CU, Mally texted.

The location would be James's camp behind the Cardinal farm. Not far from where Mally had walked with Cooper on the night of the powwow. That meant Mallory had at least the morning to try to change . . . to change what?

The future? Forever? And how? And why? Why would she condemn the friend she loved to a life Eden didn't want?

But the danger.

The danger.

Merry had felt it too.

143, Mally texted back. Love you.

Mass next morning had never been longer. Mass seemed to lengthen in direct proportion to the proximity of Easter, until Good Friday, when it was moving but intolerable. Mallory fidgeted in her seat.

At least, she thought, paying no attention to the homily, having been all over the state-park land behind the Cardinal farm, Mally knew the most direct path to the glade, where a circle of land surrounded by trees and boundaried on three sides by caves opened under the brow of the ridges that led, more than ten miles back, toward the reservoir.

On Sunday morning, after a brief phone visit with Campbell, Mallory cornered Merry in the kitchen.

"Did you talk to Mom?" Merry asked. "Now she's saying she's going to name him Angus."

Mallory waved away the chat. She said, "Listen, Ster. This is urgent. You asked me to be you, once, at David's funeral, so no one would know who was up on the ridge with him. Today, I want you to be me. It's for Eden. It's crisis time."

Meredith didn't blink. "Okay. Nobody even noticed at Neely's party. I can't figure that. We looked so much alike when we were little but not now . . ."

"To other people, we do."

"Well, of course I'll do it."

"I have to go somewhere and you need to work for me at the store. It couldn't be easier. Just don't talk so much and do what Dad tells you. He'll never notice. I won't be all day and all night."

"Eden . . . Is this what we saw?"

"Yes, it is."

"Shusha," said Merry, using their old twin word for "take care."

"Ster, I don't care how long it takes. Just don't get hurt, okay?"

"I won't. But if I were to get hurt, you'd be the first one to know."

Tim had no idea why Mallory was so tense when he picked the twins up for a swing past the hospital. And it would have never occurred to him that Mallory was going to pretend to "be Meredith." ("It's harder for you to pretend to be me than for me to pretend to be you," Merry told her twin. "All I have to do to be you is stop talking and look mad all the time.") They all sat in the room while Campbell ate her lunch and did the obligatory inspection of her drum of a belly.

"That's something right there!" Adam shouted, pointing. "That's some kind of body part."

"I would think it's a foot, from where I can feel it," Campbell said, prodding a spot just under her ribs. The pretend "Meredith" could see the outline of some definite little appendage too, but her eyes were pulled back over and over to the clock on the wall.

Tim had said he would come back at one. But now it was two, then 2:30. "Meredith" felt like crawling the walls. She loved her mother and her little sibling-to-be. But she had to consider matters so huge and harmful; she pushed away the phrase that occurred to her: "Matters of life and death."

Finally, her father came trotting through the door.

"You're late!" the pretend-Meredith said sharply.

"That's almost the first word you've said all day, Merry. You're acting like your sister. Apologize now," Campbell said. "Dad's not your taxi service."

"It's just that I want to go skiing, and now it's going to be hard to get a couple of hours in before it gets dark."

"I'm sorry," Tim told her. "Ton of inventory came in and I didn't expect it. I just forgot everything else when I saw how much winter stuff we still have left to push. Mallory's all confused today." Campbell was tired, so Tim agreed to take Adam back to the store. He stopped at the house first to load the ski things and a backpack that Mally filled with water and sandwiches.

"Going on an expedition, huh?" he asked. "Well, darn it all. I was going to ask you if you'd come back and give me a hand. Rick's off, and I thought one of you could start opening up all those spring things. Guess it'll be double duty for Mallory."

To Mally's disbelief, Tim insisted on a quick stop at the store before driving her out to a ski path. "I just want to check on your sister. I have to keep telling her to get off the phone."

Thanks, Mallory thought bitterly. *Thanks, sis. It's life and death and you can't miss a single detail of the planning for Neely's pre-party for the girls-ask-boys formal.* All the cheerleaders had agreed to wear white—a detail that Mallory found nearly intolerably absurd.

"Dad, please. It's such a nice, warm day and pretty soon I'll be back on the field . . . I mean in the gym . . . and with choir . . ."

"Just give me a minute."

But every minute counted. And relentlessly, they piled up. Tim took a phone call. Tim signed for a few more boxes. The closer it got to the end of the day, the less time she would have to talk to James, whatever good that would do. Even if she could find his camp, he and Eden might have left by the time she could get there.

She was slumped on a skateboarding ramp display when Tim was finally ready to leave. "Don't be grumpy. Plenty of daylight left. This new outdoorswoman you've turned into takes some getting used to," he said as they got into the van. "Where do you want to be dropped off?"

"Oh, out past Eden's farm, Dad, if that's okay," Mallory said, trying to sound as vague as her sister always did. "There are some great trails back there in the state park, and I can always rush over to Eden's house if I need a bathroom or I get tired. I'll call you as soon as I'm done, or just come get me after you close up. Six is fine."

As the van pulled away, Mallory tucked her hair up under her cap.

She "heard" Meredith say clearly, *Careful, careful.*

DUEL

I t took nearly an hour for Mallory to find James's encampment—a clearing in the snow ringed by rocks and spread with straw, a deep layer of it as insulation under his tent. The setting was neat to the point of compulsiveness, his gum boots tied high and hanging from a rope, his food bag even higher.

Unable to find him or Eden, even after she gave a shout, Mallory sat down to rest and unwrapped her PB&J and her bottle of ginger water. Her muscles ached from the top-speed jump across the snow, as the shadows grew ever longer. She heard the hiss of snow before she saw a tall figure on skis crossing the trail she had just taken. He was slim and agile, more than 6'3" at least. He seemed alarmed but not unduly frightened to see her sitting on a sawn-off log outside his tent.

"James, I'm Mallory Brynn. I'm Eden's friend."

"James Sabot. I would know you anyplace. Eden describes you perfectly. I'm going to make some hot choc. Want some?"

"Sure. Never turn down hot choc," she said.

James efficiently measured water from the hanging bags, or "dromedaries," that woodland travelers used when the streams were frozen. Mallory wiggled on her log. It wasn't a subject she could plunge into. *Wait,* she told herself. *Be patient.* Patience and waiting went to war with her every instinct. Once his tiny stove was burning low, James turned on his haunches and brushed back his curly white-blond hair. James had a wide-open and invitingly friendly face. Though Mally supposed she now preferred her guys dark-haired, James was handsome in a bluff, Viking sort of way. And his gem-blue eyes were soft with concern.

"You're fidgeting. I think I know why," he said. Mallory tensed. "You're worried about Eden, aren't you?"

"It's none of my business."

"But if somebody's close to you, it's hard to just stand back."

"She's only eighteen. I know that's technically an adult. But no matter how smart she is, Eden has been pretty protected. From the real world. Do you know what I mean?"

James handed Mallory her mug. "It's one of the things I love best about her. She's not like any other girl."

"And her family! It will just break their hearts. You don't know them. Her little tiny sister and the rest. I know she loves you, but this is so sudden."

"You don't have to convince me," James said, pulling off his scarf and taking a long drink. "I tell her that nothing, I mean nothing, will change the way I feel. I'll come back. But she says if we don't go ahead and get married . . ."

"Married?" Mallory gasped.

"Yes. I want that too. At least I think I do. She's only eighteen, and I have two years or more of school. People can change a lot. But she says if we don't do this now, we might as well . . ."

"James, do you know why? Do you know about Eden's tribe?"

"I know some of their traditions. I know some of their stories. What she's told me and what I've read. Is that what you mean?"

"Do you know about the shaman in the tribe?"

"Sure. It's the woman or the man who brings the medicine . . . the good luck, right? Sort of the CEO," James said. "Eden's told me that."

Mallory was panting. Deliberately, she took a swallow of hot chocolate and tried to slow her breathing. She had lived so long in the world of impossible-as-normal that it was difficult to remember how slowly ordinary people had to work through the extraordinary. Hadn't it taken her most of a year to force herself into the facts of her new life? And yet time . . . time was short. She began again, "Did she tell you that's her?"

"Her? She's a kid."

"She's a kid but she's the medicine woman."

"Mallory, she'd have told me."

"That's why I'm here. She won't tell you. It would scare you away, and you'd be right to be scared. Because of that old tradition."

"Okay," James said reasonably. "She's a big deal in their clan. Why is that a deal breaker? And why do you look so scared?"

Mallory thought, *I can't say this.* Then she thought, *I have to say this.* "Did you ever hear that a clan's shaman, the medicine woman, could be a shape-shifter? Did Eden tell you the story of the white cougar?"

"The legend? Sure. She loves that story. It's good luck for the tribe but not for hunters who run into the shape-shifter? It's an ancient myth. I've even heard it before, from other Native Americans in New Mexico," James said. "Eden is fascinated with that kind of social anthropology. I see her doing something with that someday."

I hope you don't see it, Mallory thought.

"Some Indian people believe that it's real," Mallory said.

"What?"

"That shape-shifters are real."

"Some people believe little gray guys are locked up in an airline hangar in New Mexico."

"It's not the same thing. I don't know all about it, but tribal traditions are handed down from generation to generation."

James agreed, "Sure. Like the stories in the Bible. They're huge. They're guides to life. They don't have to be literally true to have power."

Both of them froze as they heard a cough, not quite a low growl, but definitely not human.

"Stay still," James said quietly, not quite looking up but glancing from under his eyelids. "She's a small black bear and she's interested in the food, not in us. If you don't mind giving me the rest of your sandwich." Mallory picked it up and handed it over. James threw it lightly over the top of the tent. "I'm hoping if I can make a little noise and we'll walk away quietly, she'll lose interest. If I can and if there's time, I'll let the food bag down. I'll toss over some of these granola bars I have. The only thing that worries me is she probably came out of one of those rock caves, and if she did, she has cubs. But they'd be with her. I don't see any cubs. And she's not skinny enough to be a spring bear." James got up slowly. "She's not satisfied with that sammie. I'm going to let the bear bag drop."

He undid the series of knots that held the bag fourteen feet above the ground and let it fall. The bear looked up, its close-set eyes blank of emotion, with no interest in the food bag. She laid her ears back and soundlessly popped open her jaws. "Oh. Wow. Now she's letting us know we're too close, and we're going to start backing away. If she follows, we're going to be loud and show our teeth and say, 'Go away! Go away!' Don't look her in the eyes. But we're not at that point yet," James said softly.

The bear shambled a few feet toward them.

James and Mallory backed up.

"Take off your skis, because now we're at that point," James said. "Get behind me." He began to shout and wave his arms in huge circles. "Go! Go away, bear! Go away!" But the bear came closer and looked larger. She shuddered and scrabbled at the ground. "I don't know what's with her. She's acting too strange."

Mallory began to back up quickly.

"Don't! Go slow," James cautioned, looking back over his shoulder at Mallory. The bear trotted a few steps closer, forcing James and Mallory against the cliff wall.

It was at that moment that Eden came out of the trees just to Mallory's right. Carrying a large duffel over her shoulders, she wore her fringed shawl tied over a white parka and dark jeans. On her feet were her beautiful lace-up boots of white deerskin. When she saw James, her smile lit the gathering dusk in the gloomy clearing. Their red sleeping bag, hanging on the line, caught the last sunlight like a beating heart. Eden rushed forward, then stumbled to a stop. She dropped her duffel in the snow.

Mallory saw her shake her head once, and a grimace of pain creased her face.

Although she would never forget what she saw next, Mallory also would never quite be able to describe it.

Eden virtually melted and re-formed, like a tall and beautiful candle. Her dark hair swept up into thick pointed ears and a ruff of russet-tipped fur above the broadening pale sweep of forehead. Instantly, the white parka dropped away as powerful shoulder muscles and a massive, graceful feline chest formed. A thick and sinewy haunch appeared from Eden's strong, slender hip. The tang of the cat rose on the wind as did its inquisitive, otherworldly yowl. As the white puma sprang, time slowed to an unbearable suspended arc.

Transfixed, Mallory found even breathing an effort.

It was in that span of seconds that seemed to last an hour that Mallory grasped a single, paralyzing thought: She alone had seen Eden shape-shift—the emotional response to the threat and the full moon a combination that Eden was helpless to resist.

James's back was turned.

It was Mallory who would have to die or break the ancient chain.

Then the cougar fell on the black bear and a snarling, roiling tangle of black pelt and white limb collided—the puma striking low, the sow on her back legs slicing the air. Bleating, the bear closed its jaws first on the puma's head and then, as the cat wheeled to strike at the bear's exposed belly, raked a claw across the puma's thigh, opening a bright red rivulet of blood on the snowy coat. Back and forth the animals wrestled, one losing ground only to lunge back with renewed ferocity. Finally, the puma's greater size prevailed. The lion placed herself between the bear and James, driving the bear back, up the ridge, leaping and lashing as the bear bent low to protect her throat.

Mallory scarcely noticed Cooper leaping through the snow from the trees, racing along on snowshoes, his rifle cradled in his arms. Seeing Cooper, the bear turned and scuttled up the ridge trail.

In the silence, the lion's ragged breath was the only sound.

The puma turned, its great chest heaving, dark with snow and sweat, smeared with blood.

She faced Mally.

Cooper's rifle hung, useless, at his side. James started forward, raising the log he still clutched.

Mally shrieked, "No! Don't touch her. No one! Just wait!" She held her hands out, palms up. The puma's golden eyes seemed to droop, almost drowsy, as she approached Mallory. She yawned, spent. "Eden," Mallory breathed, a whisper no one could have heard at a distance greater than a foot, but which Meredith, a dozen miles away, did.

Hearing it, Merry covered her eyes with her hands. She too said, "Eden."

The golden eyes were for a moment those of Mally's friend.

If there is a way that whatever I have been given lets
me look over you, I'll do that from afar, Little Sister
of the Dark. If there is a way. From afar . . .

"Don't leave me," Mallory pleaded. "Edie, don't leave me all alone."

As she watched, the mountain lion turned its eyes toward Cooper, who dropped to his knees in the snow and stretched out his hands to caress the cat's back. The lion dropped her head, a long silver string dripping from her mouth, groggy with weariness. Her paws crossing delicately, she then approached James, who stood, his legs visibly trembling. The lion slid the length of its long form along James's hip, and stopping, walked back along his side, like a great house cat in the dusk. James squeezed his eyes closed. The lion watched him, its head tilted curiously, the blood on its flanks black in the fading light.

"James!" Mallory finally cried. "Don't you know her? Won't you touch her? She would have died for you!"

Bewildered, James began to back away.

"Look at her!" Mallory commanded him. "Look at her. It's Eden."

James forced himself to relax and look down at the creature. Then, slowly, he bent and lowered his head, placing a hand on each knee. The great white lion laid her own head against James's shoulder. He reached up and encircled the huge neck with his arms. A sound escaped James's throat—a word or a cry. It was too much to bear, too private to observe.

A moment later, Mally felt the bump against her hip as the lion passed her. When Mallory opened her eyes, the puma was jogging silently away, disappearing into the darkness under the cliff, toward the ridge path.

Mally gathered her senses.

"No!" she called. She could only now grasp what Eden had chosen. "No, no, wait! Cooper, make her come back. Cooper, listen!"

Cooper was beside her by then, holding her wet face against his rough jacket. "Mallory, there was only one way. It was her choice. Don't make it worse for her."

"You're so calm!"

"I'm not calm!" Cooper cried. "I'm . . . I'm numb. I think that when I go back to the house, Eden will be there, teasing me about you, asking me to go ice skating, telling Raina's fortune with pebbles in a cup. When she wrote me, I got on the bus. I grabbed my gun. I brought the rifle for the bear, not for my sister!"

"I thought you would shoot her, to wound her."

"No, never!" Cooper's hair straggled, wet, over his collar. "You know that the bear . . . I wasn't sure . . . until it left when it saw me."

"Sure of what?"

"It wasn't a real bear."

"It gouged her! It sliced her with its teeth!" Mallory told him.

"It was Bear Clan, Mallory. They were fighting for their medicine woman. Eden fought for her freedom. The bear . . . won."

"Oh, Cooper, it's my fault. I got here too late! I could have talked to her. The last time I saw her, there, inside the cat, she heard me."

"She would have heard you, but it wouldn't have made a difference this time."

"She can never . . . come back?" Mallory asked. "Please don't say that."

"No, never," Cooper said. "Not unless another medicine woman takes her place. In the oldest stories, some of the shape-shifters married human beings, and they were human for only a few days, at the full moon. But that . . . I know that's really a legend."

"But it wasn't a fair choice!" Mallory said, grabbing Cooper's shirt.

"It wasn't fair. And it wasn't a choice," Cooper said, his voice clogged with emotion. "She could never have hurt you or James."

James still knelt in the snow, his hands and arms a shield over his face.

Mallory still clung to Cooper's shirt. She pleaded, "Will she live? Will she be all alone? Will I see her? Will she have . . . someone like her?"

"I know she'll live. It's the same medicine. I don't know if we'll ever see her again."

"I can't bear to think of her all alone. And some fool could shoot her."

"I can't bear it either! Now that she knows it's forever, she'll hide. You're angry at me, but you just need someone to blame! I didn't make this medicine! I didn't make this world."

"I do blame you! Not you personally, but your mother and your father and all your aunts and uncles and your grandmother! You knew this was going to happen. You sacrificed her! I wouldn't have let this happen to Meredith. You should have stopped her." Cooper flinched away from her, and Mallory wheeled and bent to rouse James.

"Do I have to go now? Should I wait for her to come back?" he asked.

"She won't come back, James."

"I don't understand."

"If I had a dime for everything in my life I don't understand, I'd be so rich I could fly away. And I would. I'd never see this dumb little town again."

"She saved my life. Eden saved me."

"And she saved my life. And my sister's. At least once that we know of. Maybe more times. How do I let her go? It's terrible for you. But she's part of my life every single day."

"I don't get it, Mallory. But I'm so sorry."

"I just want you to know. I'm not blaming you. But this is for you. You have to know that she left here because she loves you more than she loves herself. Do you know that? If she followed the legend, the lion would have . . . hurt you. And Eden would be standing here, her regular self. It's just a few weeks until soccer season. It's just a month until her prom." Mallory covered her chapped face with her hands. "Oh, Eden. How can I make this be okay? It can't ever be okay."

Mally could do no more than sit on the stump while Cooper helped James break down his camp. Mally tenderly folded the big red sleeping bag that still smelled of Eden's jasmine perfume and hugged it one last time. "Please, James. Take me home. Is your car out that way? Can you drive me into town?"

"Of course," he said.

"Come back with me, Mallory," Cooper said.

"I can't," Mally said. "Not now."

Mallory could see the tears standing in Cooper's eyes. She touched his arm before he turned back toward home. Just before she left, Mallory spotted the limp shapes of Eden's white moccasin boots. Stumbling through the wet snow, she picked them up, holding their dear weight close to her. *May you live to wear out a thousand pairs of moccasins*. The duffel, with its dainty sundresses and peep-toe shoes, she left where it sat. She watched Cooper disappear. Inside her, where love for him once stirred like a warm spring, everything had gone silent and cold. She heard only the crunch of the snow and James's labored breaths, felt only the slap of the wind as they passed the Cardinals' ring of warm windows to the ghostly white of the crushed stone road. Without speaking, James drove Mallory into town and parked across from her house.

"Was it real?" James asked her. Mallory sighed.

"Yes, James."

"Will her parents know?"

"For them, it will be as though Eden has died."

"That's how it is for me," James said.

He helped Mallory get out of his car, handing her Eden's boots and her own skis. At the last instant, she turned back, giving Eden's soft white boots to James. "She made these with her own hands, James, when she was just fourteen years old. I want them. But I think she would ask me to give them to you." James received the boots as he would have held a little child.

"Thank you, Mallory," he said.

"Good-bye James. Good luck."

"Good-bye, Mallory. She . . . she told me so much. But the most important thing of all, she kept from me."

"She did tell you the most important thing."

"No. I didn't know any of this."

"She told you she loved you. That was even more important."

Her house was dark and warm. Mally closed the door behind her, and peeled off her wet clothes. Only then did she see the answering machine light blinking.

There were six messages.

The last three told her that she had a little brother.

EVER AFTER

EVER AFTER

W ell, I felt that," Campbell said, when Mally finally arrived at the hospital. "I'm certainly no spring chicken."

Grandma Gwenny and Aunt Karin, Dad's sister, were there in the hospital room, along with Tim and Adam. Tim was "smoking" a big blue bubble-gum cigar. Adam ran to Mallory as soon as he heard her in the hall.

"I saw the whole thing! Almost! Well, from the corner of the room, not right up close! It was disgusting!" Adam said delightedly. "But he's cool. He's a neat baby."

Mallory looked down on her scrunched, elfin little brother, his head no bigger than Tim's open palm, his little fists held tightly together under his chin, as if he had a secret.

She hoped that he didn't.

She hoped it would only be Merry and her. She knew Grandma had predicted that one day it would be she, Mallory, who had the twin daughters that came in every generation of their family. Aunt Karin had been a twin, but her twin was lost in a miscarriage before she was born. Being a mother herself was something Mallory could not even imagine. She had begun to see that love, all love—even that of a parent for a child—came at a price.

"Do you want to hold him, Merry?" Campbell asked. Her short hair was spiked with sweat but she looked excited, her cheeks pink and her eyes dancing with light. Mallory had forgotten. It was her twin that her parents believed had gone skiing—a few hours and a million years ago. She said, "Just let Mally show me where the soda machine is first. I'm sooo thirsty."

In the hall, Mally and Merry formally exchanged identities—Mally's flannel shirt for Merry's sleek gray sweater, the left pierced earring for the right.

"Are you okay?" Meredith asked. "I heard some of it."

"It was awful."

"Is Eden okay?"

"I'll explain later. Mom will wonder if I don't hold the baby." Back in Campbell's room, Mallory's mother placed the sweet small bundle in her arms.

The twins stood close together near the window and watched the sky darken. Merry stroked the baby's dark blond fuzz and said, "I'm so sorry. Do you think we were meant to change this?"

"If we were, we couldn't. I don't know which is worse, to live with what you changed or what you didn't."

"I hope that someday we get to see why. I can get the rest. But if we couldn't help Eden, why did we have to know?" Merry asked.

Mally kissed the baby. "Maybe because she helped us. Maybe we owed her to know."

Their mother said then, "Girls, I'd like both of you to stand in as godmother to him. Adam and my brother will be the godfathers. So if you have ideas for names, now's the time. I'm thinking Ian."

"How about Owen?" Merry asked.

"Owen Campbell," added Mally.

Campbell's eager smile broadened. "Why, I love that! What do you think?" she asked everyone. "I love that name. Owen Campbell Brynn."

"It's perfect," said Grandma Gwenny, her eyes telegraphing a secret mirth to the girls. "It's just the right name."

"And he's right as rain," Campbell boasted. "Only five pounds and two ounces but strong as a little pony."

The door opened, and first Bonnie came into the room, with Kim following her.

"Oh, Cam, congratulations," Bonnie said. The two women held each other for a long time. "He's beautiful."

Campbell said, "I thought I would feel completely terrified at the idea. Maybe it's hormones, but I think I'm going to do just great."

"I used to want to adopt a baby. Even before David died. But I'm so old," Bonnie said. "And so tired. And Dave would never allow it."

Kim said, "Mom, you're still young. You look years younger than most moms." She lied bravely about Bonnie's looks—as a good daughter should, both twins thought.

"You wouldn't be embarrassed? At school?" Bonnie asked. "If we had a baby like Mally and Merry?"

"Come on! I'd be crazy about a new baby," Kim said. "I don't mean we could replace David. But . . . we have to live, Mom."

Campbell spoke up, "I sure wouldn't mind not being the oldest mom at the preschool. You're three years younger than I am. And if I'd adopted him, I wouldn't have all this baggy, saggy . . ."

"That's enough information, Mom," Merry told Campbell. "It may just be biology but don't go into it."

"Hmmmm," Bonnie said. "I could just eat him up."

"His name's Owen," Tim put in. "His godmothers here named him."

"I think he named himself," Mallory said. They all shared a grin. And then Mallory asked, "Mom, do you care if I ride home with Kim and Bonnie? I think I'm coming down with something. I'll come back after school tomorrow."

"I'm going to raise him to play three sports," Adam said. "You don't have to help."

"And you'll love the nice green diapers," Merry put in. To Mallory she said softly their word that meant love and understanding, "Giggy. Text me if you need me. Grandma's going to stay with us—like we were two years old."

"Everyday I wish we were two years old," Mallory said. She smiled at Kim, who looked a little more like the gentle girl they'd known long ago.

Before.

There were so many times Mally now had to think of a "before."

She wondered about after . . . and all the afters to come.

"Well, I was the only one here when he came," Adam was telling

Aunt Karin. "Dad was in Deptford taking a delivery. He didn't even get here until he was out! I guess I'll be special to him." Aunt Karin agreed. Mallory knuckled Adam's head. Her own head weighed a hundred pounds. All she could think of was sleep. She kissed her parents and Grandma and told Merry they'd talk later.

When Bonnie and Kim dropped her off, she saw the envelope between the door and the screen.

She knew it would be there.

She'd had enough of sad messages.

> *Dear Mally,*
>
> *I can't stay. I don't have the courage to watch my parents go through this. I don't have the courage to say good-bye. I acted like a man but it's an act. I have a lot of growing up to do. I may come home next year. I know that I'm needed. But I'm going to have to wait to decide that until this sinks in. You're going to be a beautiful woman. Maybe I'll be here to see that. Please stay my friend. Please listen for Eden with your spirit. Please forgive me.*
>
> *Love,*
>
> *Cooper*
>
> *PS. This was meant to be a Christmas present that I never gave you. I'll wear the gloves every day and pretend you're holding my hand, okay? That's pretty sentimental for me. I know you probably made one of these at camp when you were a kid, but this*

is a real one my uncle made of white gold with your
birthstone. It's not fragile. You can wear it all the
time. Of course, it's a dream catcher. It's a dream
catcher made by an authentic Indian and guaranteed
to keep nightmares away. I don't know how effective
it is with other dreams, however. But we can hope for
the best.

Still in her long johns, Mallory fell asleep with the card under her cheek and the necklace in her hand. Down she went into the well of sleep, and when the alarm rang, she couldn't get up. Every part of her ached—her arms, her head, her legs. When she thought of the buzz at school, everyone asking about Eden Cardinal dropping out so close to the end of the year, she wanted to sleep forever. For only the second time in two years, she wanted to be called in and asked Grandma Gwenny to do it. She slept for nine more hours.

When she woke up, the imprint of the silver dream catcher on its chain was etched in her palm like her sister's scar.

INTO THE LIGHT

INTO THE LIGHT

On Saturday, although she still ached, Mallory felt like a smaller, paper-doll version of herself.

She was careful, washing her face in slow, circular strokes and examining her skin texture. It was good, she decided—no visible pore structure. She patted Vaseline on her lashes. And then she didn't know what else to do. A day in the cold had tightened her skin to the point that she felt she might split if she smiled . . . that or explode in a thousand quarter-inch squares of freeze-dried freckles. She rummaged among Meredith's two solid-packed drawers of entirely identical jars. SPF15 sunscreen. She'd heard of its virtues. And she didn't need a map on her face of all her sins, all her hopes, all her failures—not even of all her days spent lying on her back in an inch of water at noon up at the camp.

Mallory pulled on leggings and, for some reason, her short black skirt and the red-and-gray sweater and shirt she'd bought with

Eden. She pulled her hair back in a clip and touched her lips with gloss.

Now she really was all dressed up with nowhere to go.

And though it was cloudy, she even had on sunscreen.

She fastened the dream catcher around her neck on its long braided silver chain. The garnet was as red as a drop of blood.

When she stepped out to get the mail, Drew was shoveling the walk.

"What's the occasion, Brynn? You trying out to be your sister?"

"I don't know what's the matter with me. I think I changed overnight from a pumpkin into . . . into a gourd," Mally said. "I've got a new little brother, though. Came early but he's okay."

"I heard. Tim told me when you were sick."

"I wasn't sick. Just beat."

"I heard Eden moved, out to live with some aunt someplace," Drew said.

"Yeah. Guess Ridgeline's too small for almost everybody."

"Too small for Pam. She met a guy at Ohio State when she went for orientation."

"She dumped you? Drewsky! A pre-prom dump is harsh. Did you rent a tux already?"

"In fact I did. Gray cutaway."

"That must have been eighty bucks. Will they give you a refund? Oh, but they altered it, right? I'm sorry."

"What are you gonna do, Brynn? She was going to the great wild west out there anyhow. It never would have lasted. She sure was a babe, though."

"And nice. She's a nice girl," Mally said. "I gotta go in. I'm freezing. Want to watch some soaps?"

"I live for it," Drew said. "I'd rather shovel every walk on the street. Want to play laser chess?"

"I'd rather have a new nostril," Mallory said affably.

"What about pizza tonight? I can bring a bunch home. I'll even buy," Drew said. "That's how decent a guy I am, if I do say. A truly decent guy."

"You get it free, so we'll be the judge of that," Mally said.

Then Drew asked, "So, did you ever feel really curious about junior prom? From a sociological standpoint?"

"Not in my wildest, well, dreams. I'm sorry, though. I did trick you, but one thing you have to know is, I didn't. I really didn't."

Drew leaned on the shovel. "After a while, I figured it was some nuts Brynn thing that had to do with saving Kim Jellico or whatever. Some evil-eye thing I didn't want to know about."

"Trust me. You don't want to know about this." Mallory pressed the heel of her hand against one eye. "Are you asking me to go with you to the prom? Because if you are . . . love to. Thanks. I'm not allowed to date. But I'm making an exception on my own."

"You sure you want to get that dressed up?"

"Hey! It will make my sister crazy. I can borrow something from Neely Chaplin. She probably has nine or twenty designer gowns. We'll show 'em how it's done, okay?"

"I even took ballroom dancing lessons at the mall," Drew said.

"Well, my dad taught me when I was eleven. We'll cut a rug, like my grandpa Art says when he dances with Grandma. I know my mom is going to say I have to be home by midnight, though."

"That's fine." Drew smiled. "I have dinner reservations at Appetito! Don't borrow a *white* dress. I've seen you eat."

"Why, Drew, don't you know women don't really eat?"

"I forgot that. I forget it every time you eat your pizza and mine too. Say, is *Cooper* going to mind?"

"Actually, Cooper's back in Boston. He's not really in the picture."

"Well, I'm sorry. Sort of," said Drew.

"I am too. Sort of. But in another way, I'm relieved. Is that possible? Can you feel relieved at the end of something you didn't want to end?"

"I don't know," Drew said honestly. "I felt that way about Pam. Really, really lousy. But also free. Maybe it's a thing about being young. You can still start over. Not like if you were our parents' age. Maybe it's like payback for zits and constant nagging and having to go to school all the best years of your life."

"True. If you were old, you'd probably crack up over Pam."

"Over a cheerleader? Not so much, Brynn."

"Well, her loss is my gain, or something like that. Right? I'll be your rebound date."

"Well, I promise not to break your heart."

"Can't. Been done," Mallory said.

"Cooper?" Drew set his jaw.

"No, when my cat ran away," Mallory said. "Seems like a long time ago."

"Must have been. I don't even remember you had a cat."

Mallory sighed in a gust. "I'll never forget her. But she was just passing through."

LITTLE SISTER OF THE DARK

P redictably, Tim picked the day of the prom for the first formal family portrait of Owen at home.

"Please say it's casual," Mallory begged. "Please say I don't have to get formally dressed twice in one day."

"It's casual," said Uncle Kevin, whose friend, Leo, was the photographer. Everyone wore jeans and bright sweaters. Campbell asked them to group around her—on top of her if possible.

"Only my eyes look okay," said Campbell. "The rest of me is like Moby Pickle in this green sweater."

Aunt Kate styled them like a still life.

"Four kids!" Tim kept saying.

"Fortunately, people will always need soccer balls and sweat socks," Campbell told him.

"And family practice physicians," Tim added.

Leo took a few hundred shots and then beamed. Campbell began to feed the baby.

"You did a great job, champ!" Tim told her.

"I don't recall you even witnessing the title bout this time," Campbell reminded him.

Mallory began pulling on her sweats for her run, but Campbell stopped her.

"So does your going to the prom tonight with Drew mean it's over between you and Eden's brother?"

Mallory said, "Yes. I guess."

Campbell said, "I'm sorry. But when she ran off with that older man . . ."

"She didn't do that, Mom. She went to stay somewhere else. She has family everywhere, even in Canada. It's over between Eden and James." Mallory figured that she had said the gist and not quite told a lie.

"Well, I'm glad. He was too old for her."

Mally admitted, "I'm not glad. It's like she was punished for something she didn't do."

"I know you'll miss her terribly, Mally," Campbell said.

"I don't even think I know how much yet," Mallory said. "I'll miss them both." She remembered standing in the snow, her face against Cooper's wet coat, the smell of the green-heart evergreen. She saw Eden whirling alone in her moonlit dance.

Mallory decided that she would see Eden that way forever.

She went upstairs to get her sneakers.

Merry was finishing her French. She said, "Ster. That necklace. It's beautiful."

Mallory held it out and admired its delicate web, the slender hatchwork within the circle, the feather intended to drive beautiful dreams to whirl above her bed. "It's a memento. A kiss-off gift. Not that Cooper was mean about it. He wasn't. But I guess he couldn't really handle what happened to us." Again, Mallory felt empty, like a skin. If someone shook her, her small, dry heart would rattle against her ribs. "He says he'll come back maybe. But I know he won't."

"Oh, Mallory. I didn't know Cooper was . . . over."

"Well. Anyhow. I'm going to the prom, huh? Did you give Neely my note? Thanking her for the dress?"

"She was glad to do it. She just wants a picture."

"There'll be no pictures," Mallory said.

"I don't think Drew's mom is going to go along with that. It's his junior prom," Merry said.

Mallory snorted and went for her run. Up she went into the hills, alert for a flash of white, listening for the crisp of a broken bush. But she heard nothing, even though she went to the top of the ridge and waited until the sun was too close to the horizon. She had to race for home, race through her shower, and force herself to slow down while she went through the painstaking steps of putting on her eyeliner, smudging it, smudging it too much, daubing it off with baby oil, putting the white primer goo on again.

Merry was able to endure it for only five minutes.

"You're driving me crazy! Let me put that stuff on!" And so, Merry took over, the brushes magic wands in her artist's hands. "Now your hair. A messy updo with lots of wispy stuff?"

"Negatori," said Mallory.

"Okay, a French braid with a clip." With her dark hair braided tightly against her head and a swirl of silver over it, and with Neely's mermaid of a Vera Wang sheath dropped down over her head and both twins' garnets in her ears, Mallory obediently let her sister soldier-walk her over to the mirror. "My creation!" Meredith said.

And Mallory said, "Wow."

She looked like herself, only less and more. She looked twenty. She looked newborn. She looked white hot. "I didn't know they made tight dresses this small," she said to Merry.

"It was Keira Knightley's," Merry said, lowering her voice. "Or some English movie star's. They had it shortened. It cost, like, two thousand dollars in a charity auction."

"Oh, take it off, fast! I can't breathe on it! I can't breathe in it, as a matter of fact! I have bigger boobs than Keira Knightly?" Mally cried. "What if I wreck it? What if I sweat?"

"Only you would say that," Merry told her. "You put on deodorant twice! Plus, it's insured. And it doesn't even touch your pits."

"Well, okay. Geez, Merry. This should be you."

"I'm off men," Merry said. "But yes, it should be me. Put your shoes on."

"I can't bend over," said Mallory. So Merry fastened silver sandals with minute heels on Mallory's feet. Together, they walked downstairs. Tim mimed a heart attack. Drew, who was already there, talking to Adam, turned around. In his gray cutaway, Drew Vaughn looked like an old-time movie star. And whatever remark he had prepared wouldn't come out of his mouth, which wouldn't stay closed.

"Drew, flies are going to fly into your mug," Campbell said. "You knew she was pretty."

"I can hold three full-size pizzas in one hand," Drew said.

"I'm in awe," Mallory told him. She smiled. "Not of you. Of the pizza skill."

"These days I'm always saying things I never imagined I'd say. Brynn, you're gorgeous."

"Thank my sister. It's all painted on."

"Some things can't be painted on."

"To the Green Beast," said Mallory.

"My dad lent me his Lexus," Drew said. "And my mom wants to take several hundred photos."

"Told you," Merry said.

Campbell got out her own camera. "That's good. Then she won't mind if I do. I might not see Mallory this clean again until her wedding day."

Mrs. Vaughn made them pose next to the lilac bushes, the fireplace, the waterfall in the backyard, the car, and the picket fence. Drew finally said, "Mom. Halt. You'll have us driving out to the water tower next."

When they escaped, Drew said, "I'm actually looking forward to dancing after that. Ordeal by digital."

But they ate first, although Mallory had to confess that she couldn't finish her cannelloni or she'd bust out of the fabled gown. Fortunately, Drew had grieved over Pam Door, so his waistband was a little loose and he was able to finish her portion. Just before they turned into the school drive, Drew pulled over to reach into the backseat and give Mally her corsage, a black orchid with a silver band.

"It's what your name means," he said.

"My name means unlucky," Mallory said, as he slipped it over her wrist.

"I don't call you Mallory. Brynn means dark. But tonight, you're anything but."

And Drew kissed her. It wasn't her first kiss, but somehow, Mallory didn't think of Cooper. She reached up—far up—since Drew was taller than her father and let her arms rest lightly around his neck. She kissed him back and something thrummed between them that was almost like a promise and almost like a memory. Carefully, Drew released her. But Mallory put her chin up and kissed him again, not just for all the times he had made her feel safe, and loved, and home, but because he was cute and funny and smart and she felt like kissing him. She could feel his body's surprise as he pulled her closer. It was, like her mother always said—just biology—and pretty terrific. Oh, Mallory Brynn, what a girl you've become, she marveled!

"Let's go dance," she said at last. "We'll be the only people who know how."

The gym was decorated on the theme of Old Hollywood. Life-size figures of Audrey Hepburn and Marilyn Monroe lined the walls between movie posters. Couples posed for photos in someone's 1950s Thunderbird parked under an arch of neon. Mallory and

Drew made up stories about each of the couples—who was here on a pity date, who would end up getting married, who would break up by the end of the night.

At midnight, when Drew dropped her off, kissing both her eyelids, Mallory was as tired as she'd ever been after any run. She'd had a blast and was almost regretful that she wasn't allowed to date for another year.

Meredith was waiting up, and, obligingly, she and Mally texted the known universe with pictures that compared how much more beautiful Mallory looked than Pam Door—although Pam had been named prom queen.

U NO WHO REALLY WAS, Neely texted.

UR DRESS WAS, Mally replied.

She decided to shower again to remove the layers of makeup and hair gel, and when she reached up to unclasp her necklace, she panicked.

Had she worn it?

Of course not.

It wouldn't have gone with her dress.

But had she removed it? Where was it on her dresser? Meredith's dresser was a tangle of jewelry, photos, and makeup. But Mallory's was empty.

Where was it?

Mallory clutched her throat. She pulled her T-shirt up off the floor and shook it. "Merry, my necklace is gone. I had it on tonight or at least when I went running, and it's gone, Mer."

"Maybe it's in the hamper with your soccer junk from last night.

Don't go psycho. I'll vacuum in the morning. And you didn't have it on. Just our earrings and the clip in your braid. It could be anywhere."

"Where it is, is somewhere on the path. I know it. Somebody already has it. I should never have been wearing it. Not to run. It was too nice a piece of jewelry for that. And it was the only thing I have left of Cooper. Maybe the only thing I'll ever have. I'm going to bed."

"I'm sorry, Ster."

"I'm sorry too."

They carefully restored Neely's dress to its garment bag, and Mallory again anointed her face with another kind of cream she found in Merry's drawer. Then she fell into bed, muscles aching from the run and the dance, feet throbbing from the unaccustomed shoes, and punched her pillow to just the right softness.

She told the visions of Cooper's chin and Drew's broad shoulders to get lost and prayed not to dream.

But she did, and in the dream, she saw Eden.

Eden was wearing her ceremonial white deerskin dress, her hair in tiny plaits that sparkled with black and silver beads. Her feet were bare, and she stood in a pool of sparkling, sunlit water. In her hand, she held Mallory's necklace. Sadly, gently, she nodded and smiled.

Good-bye, Mallory thought. *Be safe.*

She woke up solemn. It truly was the end of something.

Still, for weeks, Mallory searched for the dream catcher on every run she took, three times a week. But she never dreamed of Eden again or saw any sign of the necklace.

The Saturday after school ended, Campbell, sure she'd wrench her back or break an arch, decided to take her first run since Owen's birth.

Jog, not run, Campbell insisted. *Slow jog, like walking with a slight bounce. Like walking and swinging your arms. Slow.* She insisted that Mallory come with her. Campbell had twenty-five pounds to lose and was determined to lose it by mid-July. At this point, she said, she wouldn't wear a bathing suit in front of Adam.

"You have to hide me," Campbell said, when she passed the hall mirror. "People will wonder if I'm an advertisement for doughnuts. If I fall, call the hospital."

It was a glorious morning, the first morning with the real promise of summer held behind its back like a surprise. Although there had been a downpour just two nights before, the long, full days of sun had dried things to the texture of a freshly laundered shirt. Since early morning, trucks and minivans rumbled past the Brynns on the way to the farmers' market at the end of the road, where flower sellers couldn't shove flats of perennials into the hands of eager gardeners fast enough to please them.

"Good," said Campbell, as one of her friends trundled past with a wagon piled with rosebushes and lilies. "No one under the age of eighty will be home on a morning like this. Either they won't recognize me or they'll have cataracts." Mallory and her mother stretched and set off at a sedate trot.

But they hadn't hit the end of their driveway when Mallory had to stop to tie her shoe.

"I'll catch up," she called to her mother and knelt to make a careful double loop.

And then she saw it, in a tiny puddle of leftover rainwater that sparkled in the sun—the garnet a dot of bright blood. Eagerly, her heart quickening, Mallory tugged and finally dislodged the chain and the dream catcher, dirty but undamaged, from the oddly shaped hollow in the ground—where it had lain perhaps for weeks, as the last dregs of the long winter and muddy spring melted away. But no, she thought, it had been warm on the day of the junior prom, warm enough for her to be comfortable on her run in a sleeveless tee.

The snow had melted a month before that late April night. If the necklace had been there, she'd have seen it.

Mally's first impulse was to call out to her mother, who was gamely trudging up Pilgrim Road, to wait until she could bring the necklace back inside. She couldn't risk losing it again, not until she got a jeweler to make sure the clasp was intact. But when she studied the clasp, she saw it was closed and whole.

And so, Mally slipped the chain carefully over her head.

It was only when the necklace was safe around her neck and against her skin, cold and gritty, but gloriously in its place, that she looked down and examined the curious-looking depression in the mud just a foot off the curve of her driveway.

It had dried in the sun, holding the necklace secure in the spring mud. Only a teaspoon of water still stood in the pool, a round, scooped-out mark with five separate parts, like a palm with four thick fingers. Mallory reached down and placed her own fingers lightly against the hollow spot. As distinct in every detail as a perfect fossil, it was a paw mark twice the size of Mallory's hand.

ACKNOWLEDGMENTS

The author wishes to thank my beloved friend, physician Ann Cullison Collins, for invaluable information on emergency-room procedures and protocols.

Again, I wish to thank my Cree Indian relatives, especially my cousin Rain and my late Aunt Patricia, for their tales and sense of the magic as poignant and possible.

I thank my son, Marty, and his friends for lifting a corner of the teenage girl and my daughter, Mia, for endless round-offs and back flips in the service of literature.